C904529637

D1685170

REGGIE RABBIT

THE GHOST OF
SEAGULL ROCK

MEET THE CHARACTERS

REGGIE RABBIT

An aspiring young rabbit detective with a nose for carrots and crime.

PIPSQUARK

A brave (and sometimes talkative) parakeet and Reggie's detective partner.

GRANNY LAVENDER

The oldest of the Rabbit family and the wisest. Also the best knitter.

LETTICE

Reggie's big sister and, in Reggie's opinion, a big annoyance.

REGGIE'S MUM

Runs the family veggie stall and cooks the best carrot hotpot in Little Critter.

REGGIE'S DAD

The second best knitter in the Rabbit family.

DETECTIVE FOX

The greatest detective in Bearburgh.

NANCY

The other greatest detective in Bearburgh.

KAI

Pipsquark's birdy pal and Seagull Rock aficionado.

NORA MASQUE

An aspiring criminal mastermind
who dreams of taking over
Masque Industries.

GRANDDADDY MASQUE

Head of Masque Industries
and will do ANYTHING to be
the most powerful (and rich)
raccoon in Bearburgh.

MORBID CRAWFORD

Granddaddy Masque's head
hench-raven and Head
of Security at Masque
Industries.

ROCCO

The oldest of the Masque
triplets according to Rocco.

RICCI

The smartest of the Masque
triplets according to Ricci.

RONNIE

The oldest and the smartest
of the Masque triplets
according to Ronnie.

For Millie and Caroline, thank you for
taking a chance on me — SH

For Rob — BM

OXFORD
UNIVERSITY PRESS

Great Clarendon Street, Oxford OX2 6DP
Oxford University Press is a department of the University of Oxford.
It furthers the University's objective of excellence in research, scholarship,
and education by publishing worldwide. Oxford is a registered trade mark
of Oxford University Press in the UK and in certain other countries

Text copyright © Oxford University Press 2024
Illustrations copyright © Becka Moor 2024

The moral rights of the author have been asserted

Database right Oxford University Press (maker)

First published in 2024

All rights reserved. No part of this publication may be reproduced, stored
in a retrieval system, or transmitted, used for text and data mining, or used
for training artificial intelligence, in any form or by any means, without
the prior permission in writing of Oxford University Press, or as expressly
permitted by law, by licence or under terms agreed with the appropriate
reprographics rights organization. Enquiries concerning reproduction
outside the scope of the above should be sent to the Rights Department,
Oxford University Press, at the address above.

You must not circulate this book in any other binding or cover
and you must impose this same condition on any acquirer

British Library Cataloguing in Publication Data

Data available

ISBN: 978-0-19-278831-3

1 3 5 7 9 10 8 6 4 2

Printed in China

The manufacturing process conforms to the
environmental regulations of the country of origin.

MIX
Paper | Supporting
responsible forestry
FSC
www.fsc.org FSC™ C110497

Swapna Reddy   Becka Moor

REGGIE RABBIT

THE GHOST OF SEAGULL ROCK

OXFORD

UNIVERSITY PRESS

HIGH IN MASQUE TOWER . . .

NORA!!

YOU CALLED, GRANDDADDY MASQUE?

HAVE YOU SEEN THIS? HAVE YOU?

MY EVIL EMPIRE IS IN CHAOS. CHAOS!

WE'RE LOSING MORE MONEY BY THE DAY . . .

WITH MORBID CRAWFORD IN PRISON, HIS RAVENS ON SECURITY AREN'T EVEN DOING THEIR JOBS ANY MORE!

I'M FINDING RAVEN FEATHERS EVERYWHERE.

AND NOW, I CAN'T EVEN RELY ON THE MAYOR FOR THAT NEW CONTRACT. SHE SAYS SHE

'NEEDS TO BE MORE CAREFUL AFTER THE CARROT DEBACLE'.

DON'T THINK I'VE FORGOTTEN THAT YOU WERE RESPONSIBLE FOR THAT. IT WAS YOUR IDEA TO AIRLIFT CARROTS FROM BARGES.

THAT MAYOR IS SO KEEN TO KEEP HER SNOUT CLEAN SHE'S CLASSING ALL PETTY CRIME AS SERIOUS CRIME NOW.

IMAGINE, WE COULD ALL GO TO PRISON FOR DROPPING LITTER!

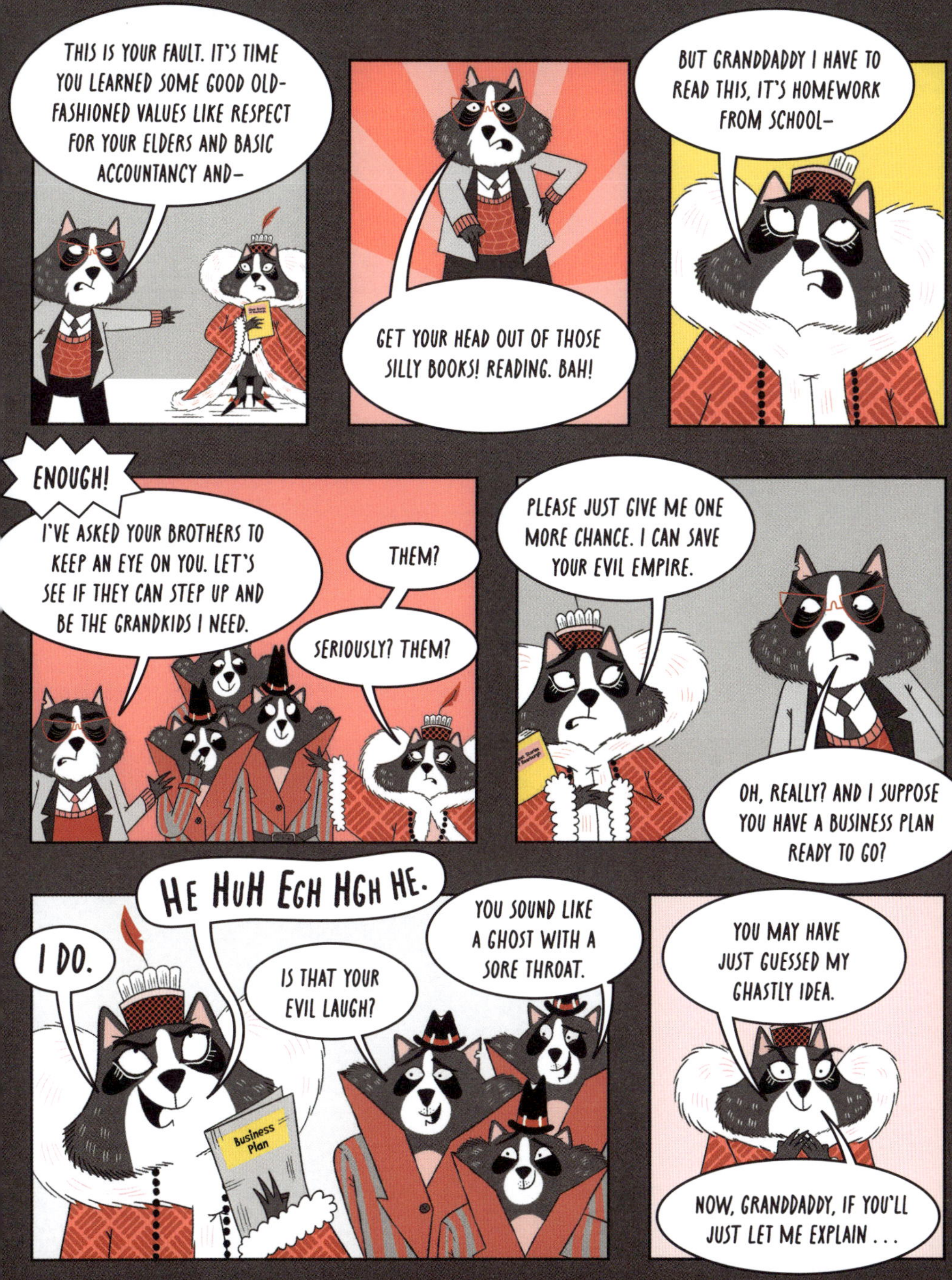
THIS IS YOUR FAULT. IT'S TIME YOU LEARNED SOME GOOD OLD-FASHIONED VALUES LIKE RESPECT FOR YOUR ELDERS AND BASIC ACCOUNTANCY AND–
GET YOUR HEAD OUT OF THOSE SILLY BOOKS! READING. BAH!
BUT GRANDDADDY I HAVE TO READ THIS, IT'S HOMEWORK FROM SCHOOL–
ENOUGH!
I'VE ASKED YOUR BROTHERS TO KEEP AN EYE ON YOU. LET'S SEE IF THEY CAN STEP UP AND BE THE GRANDKIDS I NEED.
THEM?
SERIOUSLY? THEM?
PLEASE JUST GIVE ME ONE MORE CHANCE. I CAN SAVE YOUR EVIL EMPIRE.
OH, REALLY? AND I SUPPOSE YOU HAVE A BUSINESS PLAN READY TO GO?
I DO.
HE HUH EGH HGH HE.
IS THAT YOUR EVIL LAUGH?
YOU SOUND LIKE A GHOST WITH A SORE THROAT.
Business Plan
YOU MAY HAVE JUST GUESSED MY GHASTLY IDEA.
NOW, GRANDDADDY, IF YOU'LL JUST LET ME EXPLAIN . . .

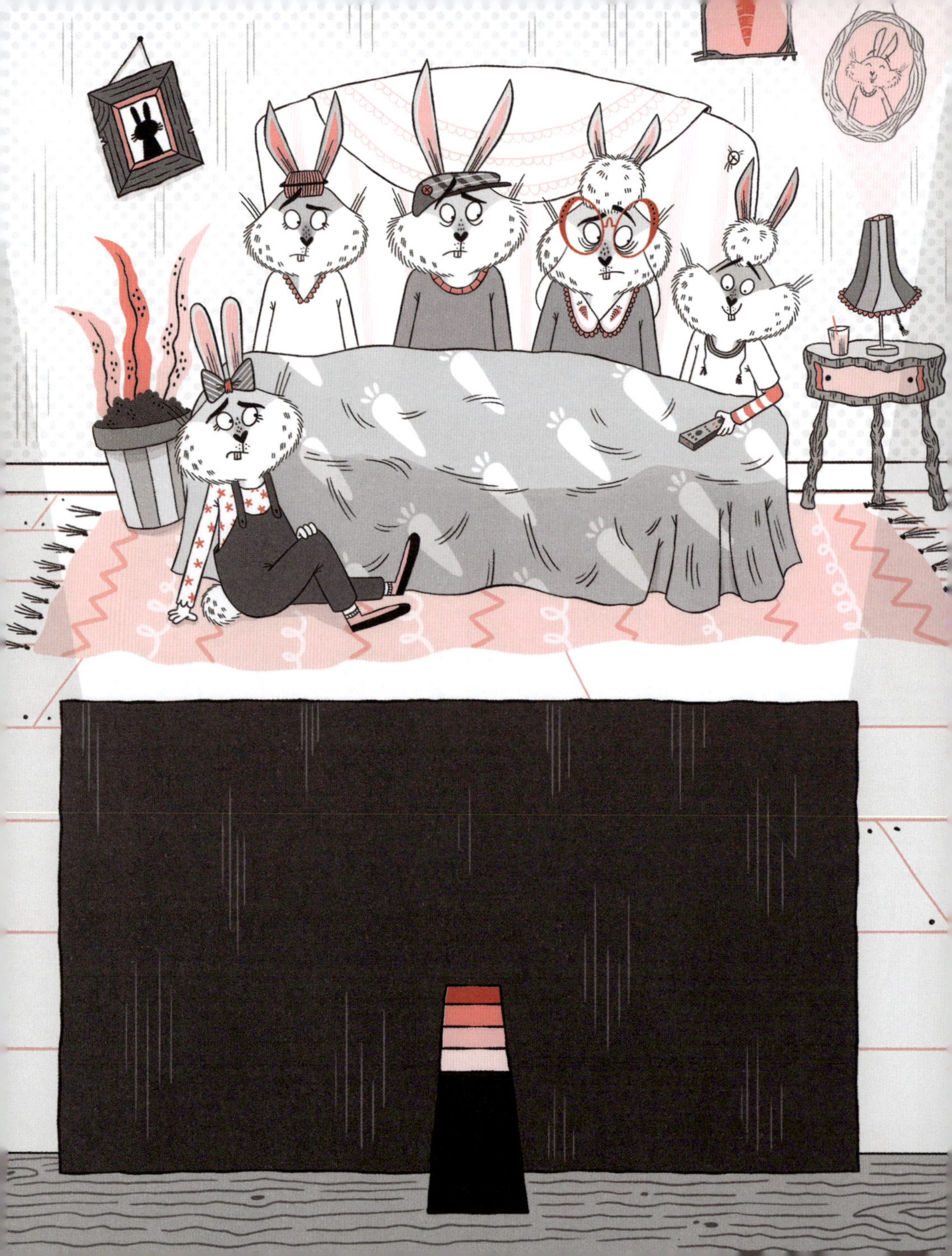

CHAPTER ONE

Reggie flicked the button on the remote control and changed the channel for the fourth time in twenty-three seconds. He was met with a chorus of groans from his family who were squeezed on the couch next to him.

'Just pick a channel,' his big sister Lettice moaned.

'Your sister is right,' Dad said. 'You've been flicking through news channels back and forth and it's making me a bit dizzy.'

'Me too,' Mum agreed. 'Seeing all the news on all the channels is not good for my nerves.'

Reggie pinged back to the news channel the Rabbit family usually watched and settled back against the plump cushions of the couch.

'I don't understand where Detective Fox is,' he said, mainly to himself. 'Who is keeping the city safe?'

It had been weeks since Reggie and his best friend Pipsquark had teamed up with Detective Fox and his partner Nancy, to solve the Great Carrot Heist. But since then, there had been no news of the great detective at all.

Reggie knew better than to assume that Bearburgh was now completely crime-free, and he suspected that the Masque family were planning their next move.

The TV screen was filled with Mayor Bear's massive head. Reggie couldn't help stifling a yawn as the mayor talked about refurbishments to the town hall and all the new apartment buildings she was planning to build. She even showed off a model of the project.

'. . . Beaver Builders will be starting with the town hall. Unfortunately, the roof is leaky and the original building is damaged as a result.'

'Isn't that the roof that Masque Industries were responsible for constructing?' the reporter asked.

Mayor Bear waved a paw as if brushing off the question. 'I don't like to play the blame game. Mayor Bear is a fair mayor! I'm here to fix problems and we have a housing problem that I'm about to fix with a host of brand-new luxury apartments.'

All eyes of the Rabbit family were on Granny, who they all thought had dozed off.

'Who does she think she is?' Granny muttered. 'She's building these flash new apartment buildings, but regular folk can't afford them!'

Reggie opened his mouth to say something, but Granny Lavender continued. 'This is exactly what happened in my day and is exactly the reason we left the city and set up here in Little Critter.'

'Little Critter's not so bad,' Lettice said, soothingly.

'It's not,' Granny Lavender said quietly. 'But it would have been nice to have a choice about leaving. We were pushed out of our homes by people like her. If anyone needs me, I'll be working on my book.' She bundled up her knitting and left the room.

Reggie's mouth fell open. He wasn't sure he'd ever

seen his grandmother this upset before.

'What's got her carrots in a twist?' Dad said.

'And what's this about writing a book?' Mum asked.

'Isn't it a story about history or something?' Lettice said.

'I think it's about being old,' Dad said, knowledgeably.

Reggie sighed. His family never paid attention—they

would all make terrible detectives.

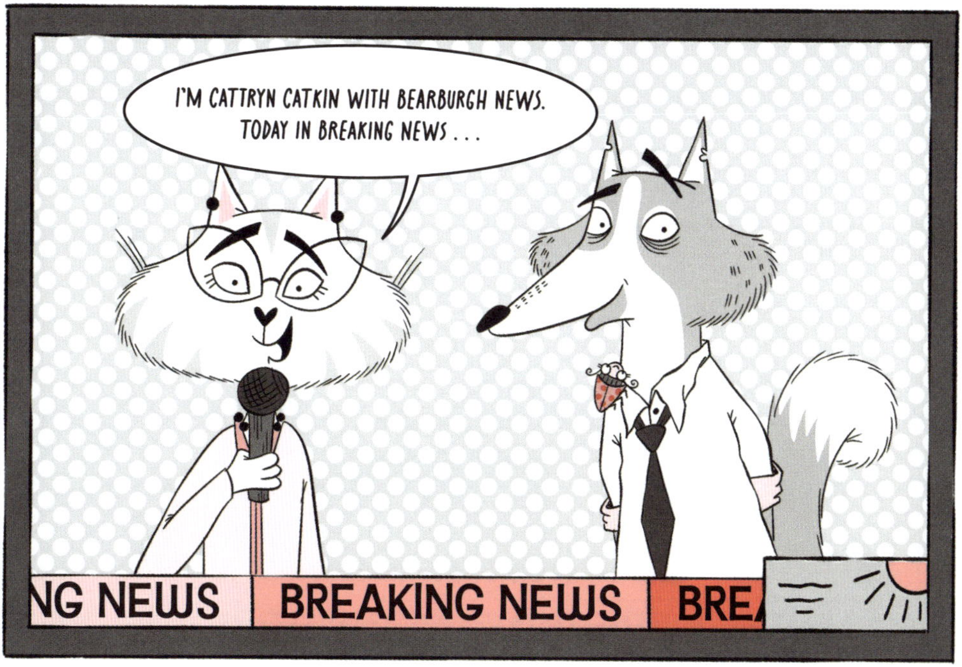
I'M CATTRYN CATKIN WITH BEARBURGH NEWS. TODAY IN BREAKING NEWS . . .
NG NEWS
BREAKING NEWS
BREA

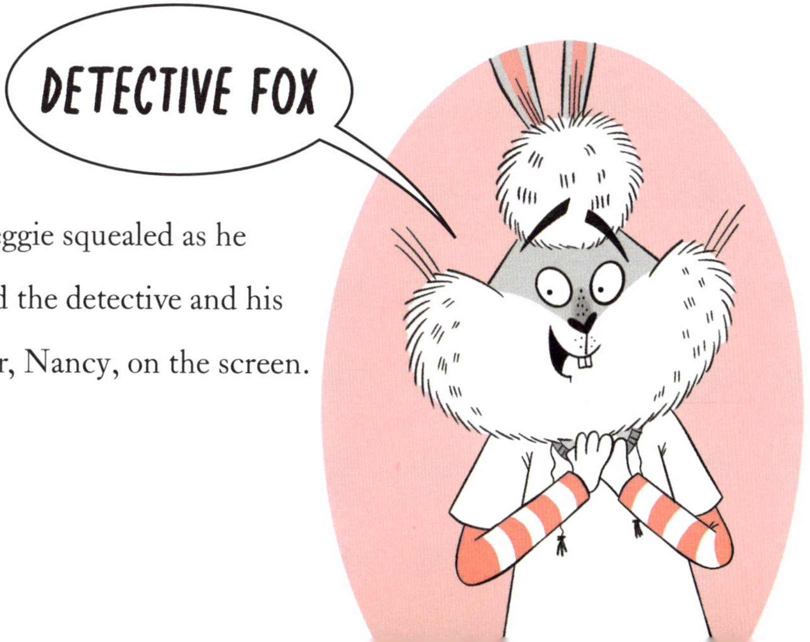
DETECTIVE FOX

Reggie squealed as he spotted the detective and his partner, Nancy, on the screen.

They were standing on a street beside Seagull Rock, a huge seagull housing estate on the edge of Bearburgh City. Reggie recognized it from photos Pipsquark had shown him of her holiday at the coast last year.

'Ooooo,' Lettice mocked, 'it's Reggie's hero!'

'Shhhhh,' Reggie hushed as the news reporter spoke

and a picture of a kind-looking old seagull flashed on
the screen.

'. . . Mr Gabbiano, a local fish and chip shop owner
and former activist, has been arrested for
selling out-of-date chips, which
we are now hearing, were more
than likely stolen,' Cattryn
Catkin reported.

On the screen the picture
of Mr Gabbiano had disappeared
and now Cattryn Catkin was
standing beside Detective Fox and Nancy,
ready to interview them. Mayor Bear was beside them,
smiling at the camera.

Reggie leaned forward, so close that his nose almost
touched the screen.

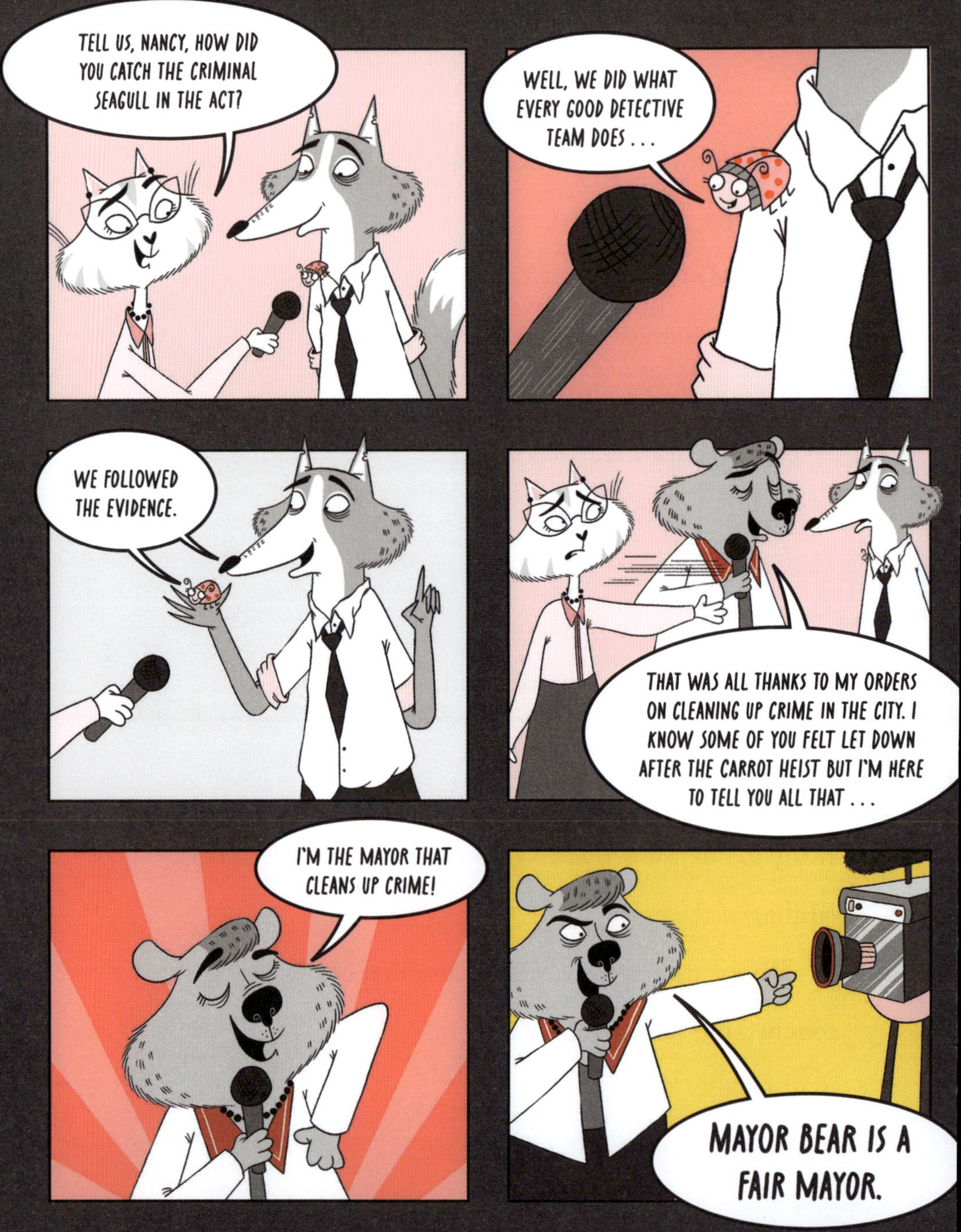
TELL US, NANCY, HOW DID YOU CATCH THE CRIMINAL SEAGULL IN THE ACT?
WELL, WE DID WHAT EVERY GOOD DETECTIVE TEAM DOES . . .
WE FOLLOWED THE EVIDENCE.
THAT WAS ALL THANKS TO MY ORDERS ON CLEANING UP CRIME IN THE CITY. I KNOW SOME OF YOU FELT LET DOWN AFTER THE CARROT HEIST BUT I'M HERE TO TELL YOU ALL THAT . . .
I'M THE MAYOR THAT CLEANS UP CRIME!
MAYOR BEAR IS A FAIR MAYOR.

The screen quickly flashed to a weather update for the coming week.

Reggie was aghast.

What was that?

How could the greatest detectives in Bearburgh, maybe even the world, be on the case of a criminal seagull who sold old chips?! What had happened to foiling master criminals? What had happened to cracking the greatest conundrums of Bearburgh? What had happened to the detectives who helped solve the Great Carrot Heist?

'You'll want to shut your mouth, Reggie, or you might catch flies,' Mum said.

Reggie hadn't realized his mouth was still hanging open in disbelief.

19

'What's so important about some old chips?' Lettice scoffed. 'I'm sure there are actual crimes that those detectives should be solving.'

'Now, now, Lettice,' Dad interrupted. 'Remember how upset we were as a rabbit community during the Great Carrot Heist? Perhaps chips are the same for seagulls.'

Reggie was unable to say a word. For the first time in a long time—maybe ever—he actually agreed with his sister.

CHAPTER TWO

'Can you believe it?' Pipsquark squawked the minute Reggie sat down at his school desk the next morning.

'I know!' Reggie replied. If anyone could understand his disbelief over Detective Fox's recent case, it would be Pipsquark.

'It's the best news ever!' Pipsquark carried on.

Huh?

'I couldn't believe it when I first heard,' the parakeet

said. 'But then I could believe it because my mum wouldn't lie to me. Well not about that. I'm pretty sure she ate some of my Halloween sweets last year while I was asleep, but she still says that it must've been rodents—'

Rodents? Sweets? What did any of that have to do with Detective Fox and Nancy?

'What are you talking about?' Reggie interrupted.

All thoughts of Detective Fox, Nancy, and fish and chips vanished from Reggie's mind. Pipsquark's bestest friend in the whole world? He thought *he* was Pipsquark's bestest friend in the whole world.

'You are going to love her, Reggie.' Pipsquark grinned. 'In fact, I'm sure by the end of the weekend, we'll be a team of besties.'

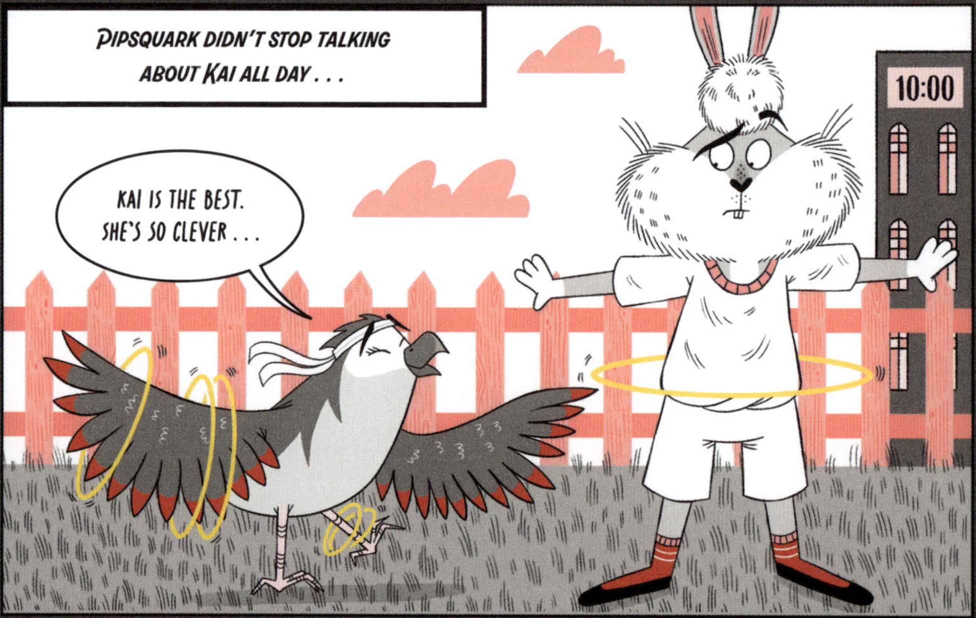
PIPSQUARK DIDN'T STOP TALKING ABOUT KAI ALL DAY . . .
10:00
KAI IS THE BEST. SHE'S SO CLEVER . . .

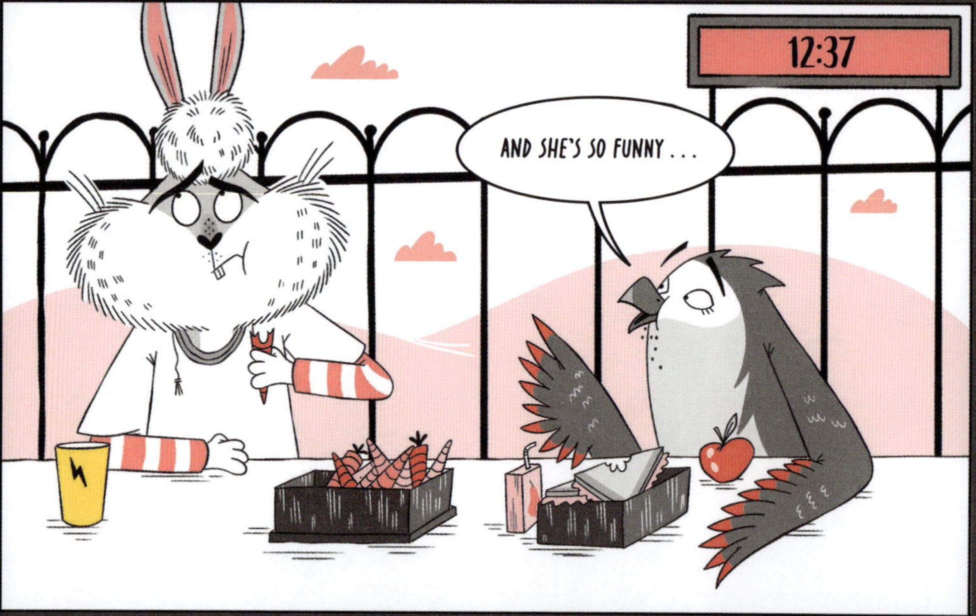
12:37
AND SHE'S SO FUNNY . . .

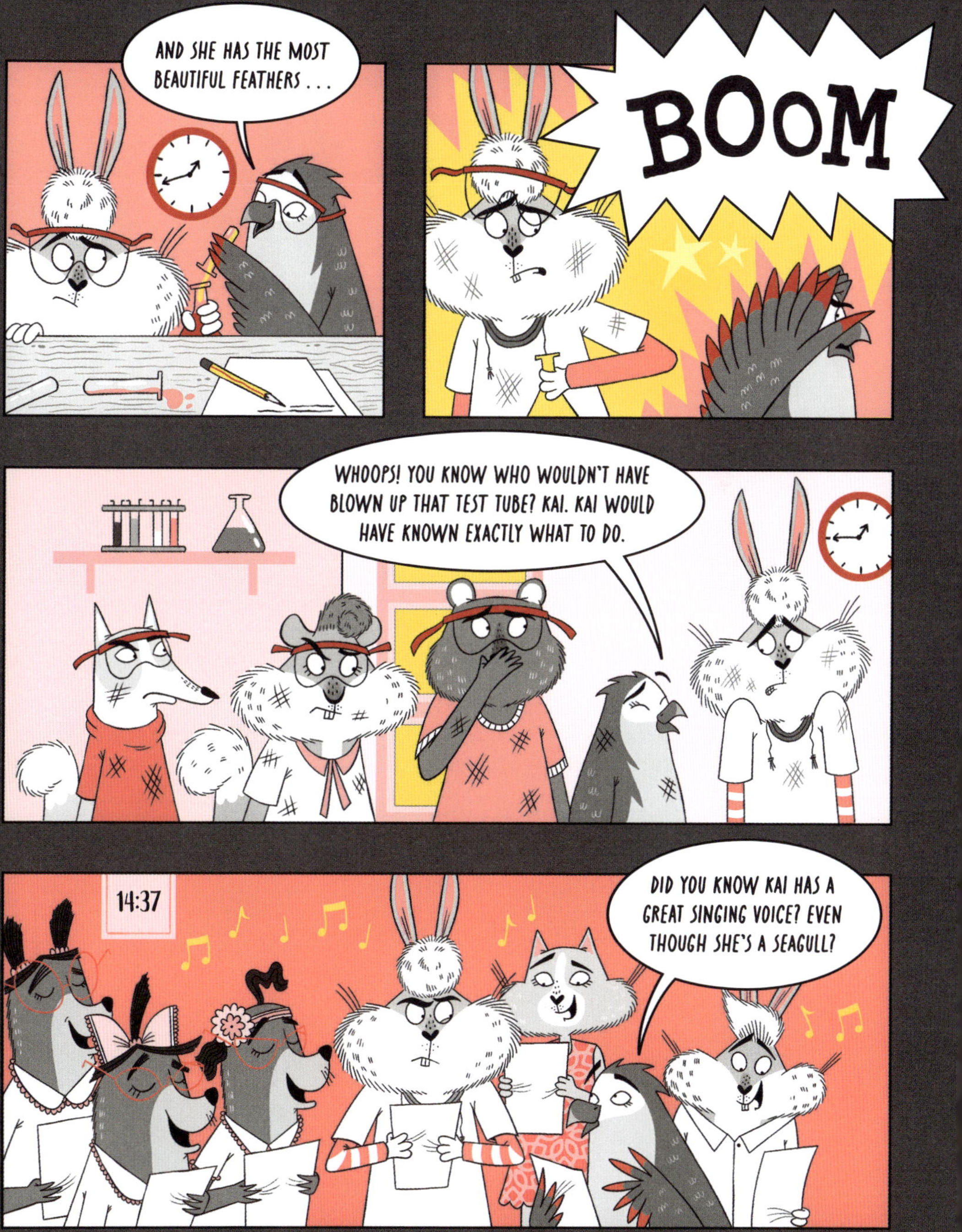
AND SHE HAS THE MOST BEAUTIFUL FEATHERS . . .
BOOM
WHOOPS! YOU KNOW WHO WOULDN'T HAVE BLOWN UP THAT TEST TUBE? KAI. KAI WOULD HAVE KNOWN EXACTLY WHAT TO DO.
14:37
DID YOU KNOW KAI HAS A GREAT SINGING VOICE? EVEN THOUGH SHE'S A SEAGULL?

TRRRITINNNG

The bell for the end of school couldn't have rung quickly enough. If Reggie had to hear one more thing about the clever, funny, feathery, singing, wouldn't-blow-up-a-science-experiment Kai, he thought he might explode himself.

He took a deep breath and trudged across the school playground as Pipsquark chattered on.

'Only, here's the thing, Reggie,' Pipsquark started

as they approached the gates. 'I really want to have a sleepover this weekend with you and Kai.'

Reggie kept his eyes firmly on the ground.

'But Mum and I don't really have the space for both of you to sleep over at our nest,' Pipsquark continued. 'Mum could only afford a small nest when we moved here because nests are quite expensive even if you are working a good job like Mum. I really don't mind, to be honest. When you live in a small space and you lose something, there are fewer places to look for what you've lost. Like last week, I lost my lucky pen. You know the one with the orange sparkly bits, though some of those have peeled off—'

'You can have the sleepover at mine,' Reggie found himself saying.

'Really?' Pipsquark squealed. 'Thank you so much,

Reggie. You are the best.'

Reggie smiled at his friend for the first time that day. He couldn't quite believe the words that had just come out of his mouth, but it had all been worth it to hear Pipsquark so happy with him.

'I'll ask Mum and Dad tonight but I'm sure it will be fine,' Reggie said. He beamed at Pipsquark and even though the smile felt forced, he definitely didn't want Pipsquark to think he was jealous of Kai. Because he very clearly wasn't. She actually sounded quite annoying.

CHAPTER THREE

The weekend arrived and Reggie was glad to see his detective skills were still sharp. When Kai arrived she was just as annoying as he thought she would be.

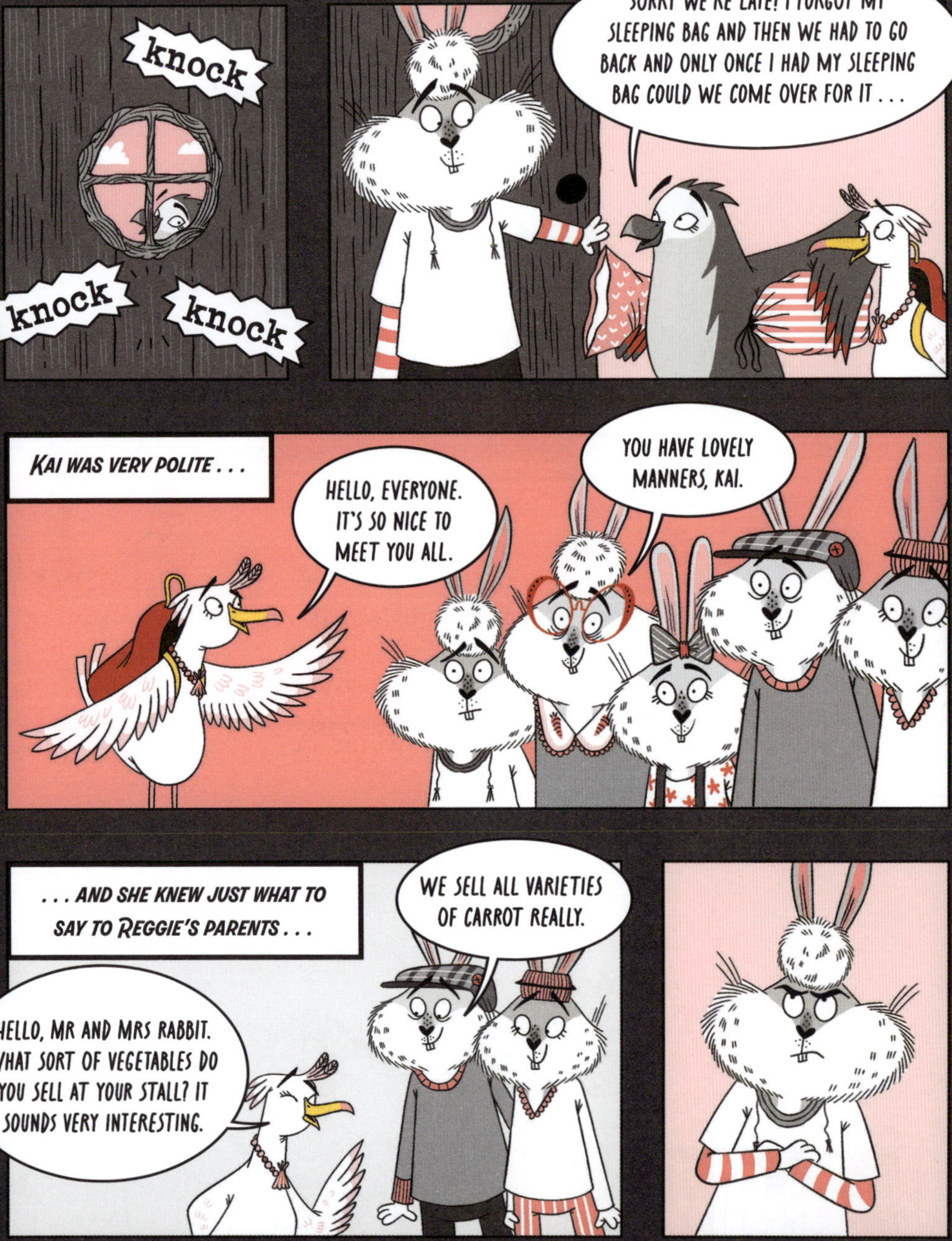
knock
knock
knock
SORRY WE'RE LATE! I FORGOT MY SLEEPING BAG AND THEN WE HAD TO GO BACK AND ONLY ONCE I HAD MY SLEEPING BAG COULD WE COME OVER FOR IT . . .
KAI WAS VERY POLITE . . .
HELLO, EVERYONE. IT'S SO NICE TO MEET YOU ALL.
YOU HAVE LOVELY MANNERS, KAI.
. . . AND SHE KNEW JUST WHAT TO SAY TO REGGIE'S PARENTS . . .
HELLO, MR AND MRS RABBIT. WHAT SORT OF VEGETABLES DO YOU SELL AT YOUR STALL? IT SOUNDS VERY INTERESTING.
WE SELL ALL VARIETIES OF CARROT REALLY.

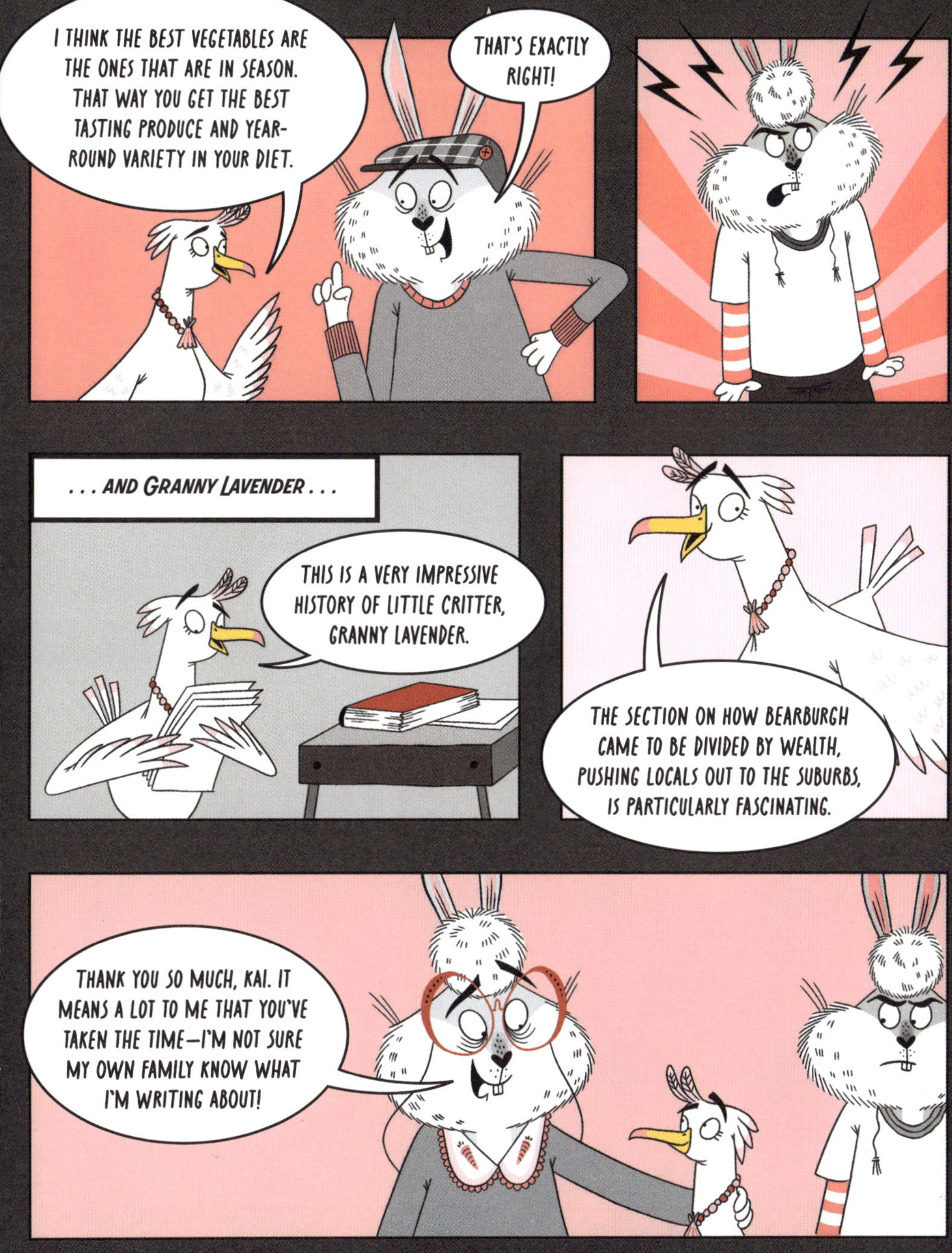
I THINK THE BEST VEGETABLES ARE THE ONES THAT ARE IN SEASON. THAT WAY YOU GET THE BEST TASTING PRODUCE AND YEAR-ROUND VARIETY IN YOUR DIET.
THAT'S EXACTLY RIGHT!
. . . AND GRANNY LAVENDER . . .
THIS IS A VERY IMPRESSIVE HISTORY OF LITTLE CRITTER, GRANNY LAVENDER.
THE SECTION ON HOW BEARBURGH CAME TO BE DIVIDED BY WEALTH, PUSHING LOCALS OUT TO THE SUBURBS, IS PARTICULARLY FASCINATING.
THANK YOU SO MUCH, KAI. IT MEANS A LOT TO ME THAT YOU'VE TAKEN THE TIME—I'M NOT SURE MY OWN FAMILY KNOW WHAT I'M WRITING ABOUT!

. . . AND OK, SHE DID HAVE A GOOD VOICE . . .

BEEEEAUTIFUL BIG EEEEEARS!

. . . BUT KAI WAS MUCH MORE ANNOYING THAN REGGIE HAD EXPECTED . . .

THAT'S MY FAVOURITE SONG FROM RABBIT POP STAR. YOU HAVE SUCH AN AMAZING VOICE, KAI.

'I think we need a new case,' Reggie said to Pipsquark later in the evening.

Kai was in the kitchen, helping his mum cook a carrot roast for dinner, and this was the first moment Reggie had to speak to Pipsquark alone. He could see it now—just him and Pipsquark working together to keep the city safe. An activity that required absolutely no Kai.

'Didn't we just solve the Mystery of the Missing Headphones?' Pipsquark replied.

'That wasn't a real case,' Reggie scoffed. 'Granny Lavender had just borrowed Lettice's headphones to listen to a new hip-hop album.'

'Do we have a case that needs solving?' Pipsquark asked.

Reggie didn't but he'd finally got her attention and he wasn't going to let it go.

'We're detectives, Pipsquark. The clue is in the name.

33

We need to go and detect. I'm sure there's a case out there.'

'We can talk about it later,' Pipsquark reassured Reggie as they were called to the dinner table.

Kai had helped make a salad and everyone agreed it was one of the best salads they had ever had. Reggie thought it was a completely bonkers idea to mix melon with kale. But he ate it because he was hungry and absolutely not because it was tasty.

'This is the best sleepover ever,' Pipsquark announced. She beamed at Reggie and Reggie returned the smile, though his jaw hurt from clenching his teeth.

'What a great meal,' Reggie's dad said. 'Thank you, Kai.'

'You know you're welcome here any time,' Reggie's mum added.

'Thank you so much,' Kai replied. 'I would love to have Reggie and Pipsquark over to Seagull Rock next weekend for a luncheon and a sleepover to say a proper thank you.'

She raised her eyebrows hopefully at Reggie as Pipsquark shrieked a loud 'yes' in reply.

'I think I might have homework,' Reggie said, coming up with an excuse on the spot. What even was 'luncheon'?

'Come on, Reggie,' Pipsquark said. 'It will be fun! You remember how to have fun, right?'

Reggie couldn't think of another excuse so he managed a small smile, though it felt more like a grimace.

'Yesss!' shouted Pipsquark. 'We're going to have the best weekend EVER!'

As the rest of his family went to bed, Reggie, Kai, and Pipsquark rolled out their sleeping bags on the living room floor. Pipsquark's comment about fun was gnawing at Reggie's thoughts. He had to show Pipsquark he was a fun friend.

'Let's tell ghost stories,' he suggested.

'Yes!' Pipsquark said excitedly.

Reggie turned down the lights with a giggle and both friends turned to Kai.

But for the first time since she had arrived, Kai didn't seem so confident. Even in the dim light Reggie could see her frowning.

'Errm, OK,' she replied in a small voice.

'I'll go first,' Reggie said. 'Has anyone heard the story

of the Headless Hopper?'

LONG AGO, IN THE TOWN OF BUNNYHOP, WHERE THE FRUIT AND VEGETABLES GREW APLENTY, A STRANGER ARRIVED IN THE TOWN . . .

HE WORE A LONG DARK CLOAK THAT SHROUDED HIS FACE AND RUMOURS WERE RIFE THAT HE HAD COMMITTED CRIMES SO TERRIFYING THEY COULD NOT BE UTTERED.

HE KEPT TO HIMSELF AND THE TOWNSFOLK WERE FINE WITH THAT. BUT THEN ODD THINGS STARTED TO HAPPEN.

EVERY FULL MOON, RABBITS CLAIMED THEY COULD HEAR HOWLING FROM THE VEGETABLE PATCHES.

AWWOOOOOOOOHHH!

THE HOWLS KEPT BABIES UP AT NIGHT AND FRIGHTENED THE ENTIRE TOWN.

ONE BRAVE BUNNY DECIDED TO INVESTIGATE AND, AT THE NEXT FULL MOON, SHE SET OUT FOR THE VEGETABLE PATCH.

AWOOOOOH!

THEY SAY SHE SAW SOMETHING TERRIBLE. A RABBIT IN A LONG DARK CLOAK, FEASTING ON GHOSTLY VEGETABLES, HOWLING AS HE CHOMPED AND CHOMPED . . . BUT HE HAD NO HEAD.

HOOOOOOOOWWWwwWWL!

HOOOOOOOOWWWwwWWL!

HOOOOOOOOooWWWWwwWL!

STOP IT, STOP IT!

Kai hurtled out of her sleeping bag and raced to the kitchen.

She ran right into Granny Lavender who was getting herself a glass of water.

'What's wrong, Kai?'

The little seagull sobbed into Granny's dressing gown.

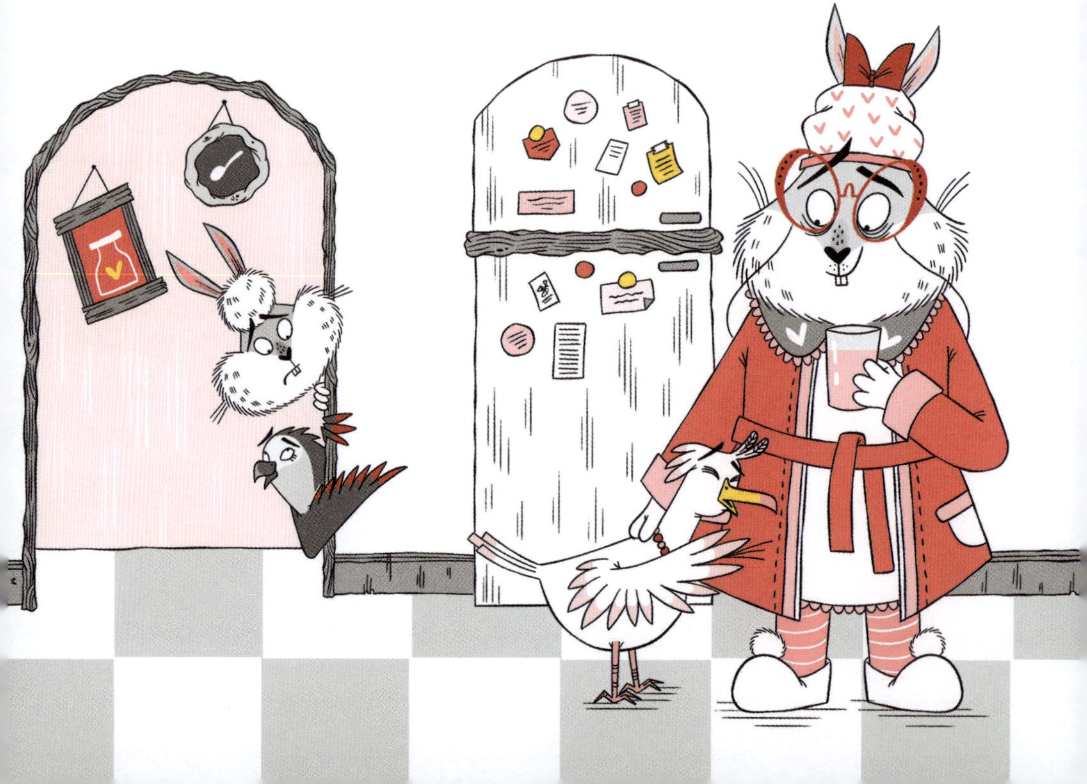

Pipsquark and Reggie were right behind. Reggie's chest felt tight. Maybe the first time he'd heard the Headless Hopper story, it had scared him a little. But he'd never seen anyone cry about it. He felt awful.

'I'm sorry, Kai,' he said, unable to meet her gaze.

'It's not your fault, Reggie,' she said, wiping away her tears.

Granny Lavender sat Kai down at the dining table and Pipsquark hugged her tight.

Kai sniffed. 'Really, Reggie,' she said. 'It's not your fault at all.'

'Why don't you tell us what's wrong?' said Granny Lavender gently.

'It's nothing.' Kai sniffed again. 'It's just me making a bald eagle's nest out of a hummingbird's.'

'Huh?' Reggie blurted.

Kai sniffled again. 'Bald eagles make the largest nests in the bird world and hummingbirds make the smallest.'

'I knew that,' Reggie mumbled defensively, though he didn't and the confused look on his face gave him away. 'I simply used the idiom to explain that perhaps I was making too big a deal of it,' Kai explained.

Reggie blinked. Why did Kai have to use such fancy words? He felt annoyed at her even though she was upset, which made him feel guilty.

Kai's chest heaved but she took a long sip of the chamomile tea that Granny Lavender had given her and seemed calmer.

'It wasn't the story,' she said. 'Not really.'

Reggie's ears pricked up. 'So what was it?' he asked.

IT'S JUST THAT GHOSTS SCARE ME BECAUSE THERE IS ONE HAUNTING SEAGULL ROCK.

Reggie's eyes widened. Ghosts weren't real! They were just made up for stories to scare little kids.

'I know it sounds silly but it's true,' Kai insisted. 'Every few days, seagulls hear terrible howls coming from the passages in our housing block. Even my mother and father have heard the howls.' She took another sip of her tea. 'Nobody believed it was a ghost at first but we've searched the whole of Seagull Rock. There's no explanation other than a supernatural being. I've read all the history books in our library and I'm certain it's the ghost of Blackbeak.'

'Who?' asked Reggie.

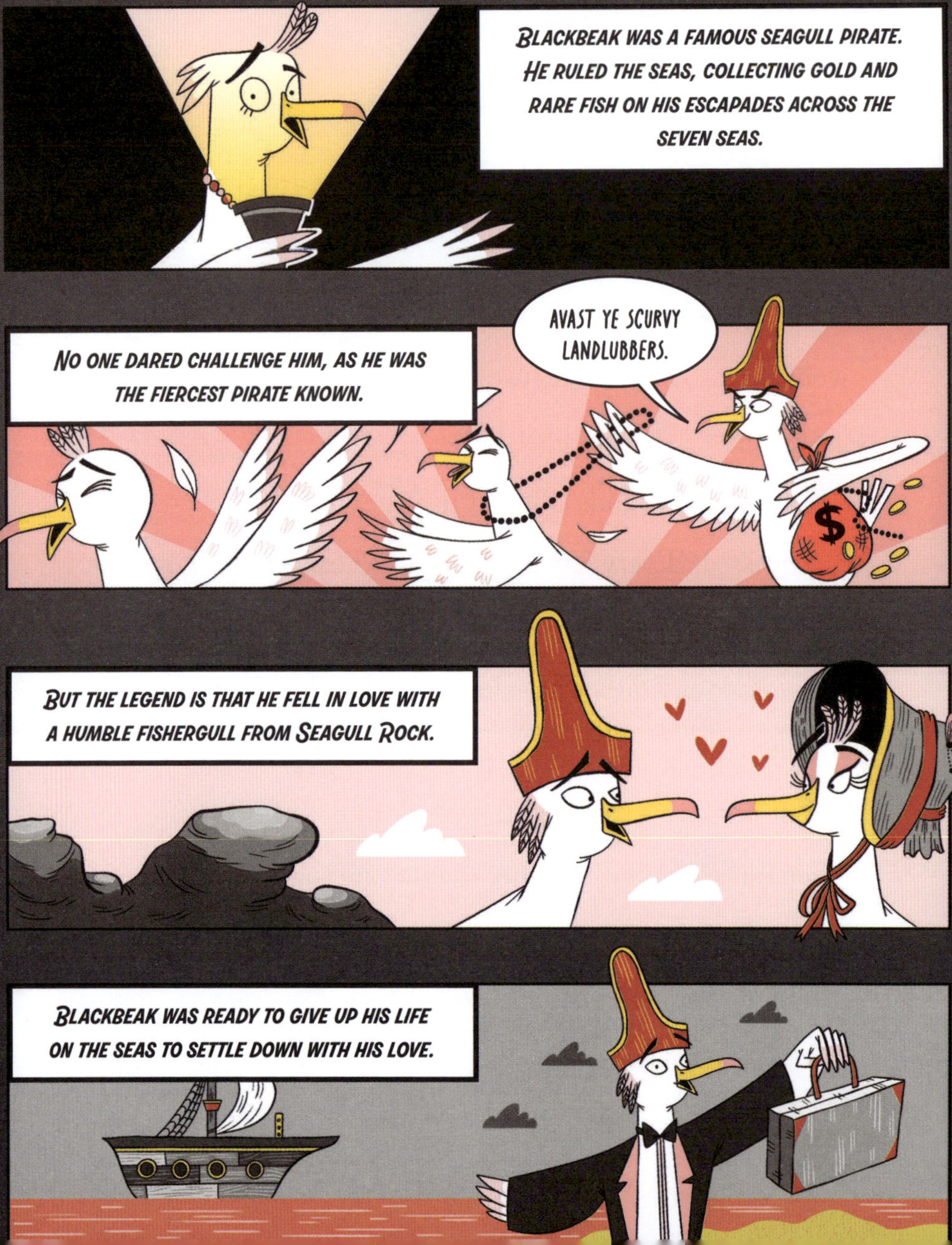
BLACKBEAK WAS A FAMOUS SEAGULL PIRATE. HE RULED THE SEAS, COLLECTING GOLD AND RARE FISH ON HIS ESCAPADES ACROSS THE SEVEN SEAS.
NO ONE DARED CHALLENGE HIM, AS HE WAS THE FIERCEST PIRATE KNOWN.
AVAST YE SCURVY LANDLUBBERS.
BUT THE LEGEND IS THAT HE FELL IN LOVE WITH A HUMBLE FISHERGULL FROM SEAGULL ROCK.
BLACKBEAK WAS READY TO GIVE UP HIS LIFE ON THE SEAS TO SETTLE DOWN WITH HIS LOVE.

THE PAIR AGREED TO MEET IN THE CAVES ONE NIGHT . . .

BUT SHE NEVER CAME.

HE WAITED AND WAITED AND THOUGH THE CAVE FILLED WITH WATER FROM THE RISING TIDES AND HIS SHIP FULL OF RICHES WAS UNGUARDED, HE NEVER LEFT THE CAVE.

BUT THE FISHERGULL HAD TRICKED HIM! INSTEAD OF MEETING HIM SHE'D TAKEN HIS SHIP AND HIS GOLD AND SAILED AWAY. BLACKBEAK MET HIS END IN THAT CAVE, AND TODAY HIS GHOST HAUNTS IT, HOWLING FOR HIS LOST LOVE.

There was silence in the room and Reggie had to use every shred of self-control not to burst out laughing.

Granny Lavender cleared her throat.

'Maybe it is the ghost of Blackbeak . . .' she said.

Reggie eyes were so wide with shock he was sure they were about to fall right out of his head.

'. . . but if I were you, I would want to be sure,' she continued. She glanced over at Reggie, her eyes twinkling. 'I think you might need someone who's good at uncovering the truth to help you,' she said.

Pipsquark smiled at Reggie. 'Well, you did want a new case, didn't you, Detective Reggie Rabbit?' she added.

'A new case?' Kai asked.

'Reggie and I are detectives,' Pipsquark said proudly.

Kai's beak fell open in amazement. 'Wow! Could you

investigate for me?'

'Of course we could!' Pipsquark said.

Reggie beamed—he could see he'd impressed
the seagull.

The idea of getting his paws on a new case and
showing off his detective skills made Reggie's tummy
tingle with excitement. Even if it meant spending another
weekend with Kai.

'Count me in,' he said.

Chapter Four

The weekend at Seagull Rock came round soon and before he knew it, it was time for Reggie to pack. He headed up to his room and shut the door gently, pulling on his detective coat. He tapped the light layer of dust off the top of his hat and pulled it snugly over his ears, as he looked at himself in the mirror.

Pipsquark was yelling all the way from the front door of the warren.

Reggie grabbed the last of his things and rushed out to his dad's car, where he squeezed into the back alongside Pipsquark.

'Let's go!' his dad cheered as he started the car.

Reggie hadn't told Pipsquark that during the week he had gone to the library with Granny Lavender to do a bit of research on the ghost of Blackbeak. He'd found a short paragraph on the seagull in an encyclopedia of myths of Bearburgh and an old storybook with faded pictures of a bird on a pirate ship.

He still thought that Kai was making a bigger deal of the old tale than she needed to—after all, he knew there were no such thing as ghosts. But he also knew that every good detective had to do all the fact-finding they could before they got drawn into a case.

'This "ghost" thing Kai was going on about is so silly,' Reggie scoffed, as he and Pipsquark looked out of the car window. 'I can't believe she made us sit through that fairy tale about pirates.'

'You didn't believe her?' Pipsquark questioned, staring hard at Reggie.

'You did?' Reggie replied, astounded.

'Sure,' Pipsquark said. 'Why would Kai lie?'

Reggie desperately wanted to tell his friend that he was sure Kai had made the whole thing up—probably because she wanted to be the centre of attention—but he'd misjudged how much Pipsquark would defend the seagull.

'Oh, I don't know,' he mumbled, and the conversation ended with Pipsquark pointing out all the Bearburgh sights she could spot from the window.

LOOK! WE'RE GOING THROUGH CAT ALLEY! IT'S NEXT TO DOG LANE AND APPARENTLY THEY DON'T GET ON . . .

'Here we are,' Reggie's dad announced as he turned left onto a sandy verge and parked the car.

They had pulled up in front of a huge cliff of apartments that rose from behind the pale tussocks at the edge of Seagull Beach. It was so huge, Reggie could barely see the top.

'Pipsquark, Reggie! You're here!' came Kai's excited caw from behind them.

'I can't wait to give you a tour of Seagull Rock,' she said, grinning.

After they dropped off their bags, she showed them
around her apartment and **Reggie** had to admit he was
impressed. The apartment itself was small but cosy. The
walls were lined with seashell-framed pictures of Kai and
her parents on their family adventures, and the home
smelt of fresh air and seawater.

Kai's room was filled with books from floor to ceiling. There was a big fluffy whale toy propped against her bed. She also had an old record player, and black-and-white posters of jazz musicians covered the wall by the doors. Reggie's nose wrinkled as he wondered why her room looked like it belonged to a boring adult.

Granny Lavender had told Reggie she thought Kai was an 'old soul', but Reggie was sure Kai was just pretending to be like an adult so she could be in charge of everyone.

There was a whole load of awards and trophies on her bedside table. Reggie's mouth fell open as he counted the many prizes Kai had won for her writing, reading, and debating.

His eyes narrowed as he spotted her spelling award and he remembered his own teacher, Mr Hare, telling him he needed to try harder with his spellings in class.

He made a quick note to himself to remember that Kai was clearly good with words and probably liked making up stories. Maybe even stories about ghosts . . .

A high-pitched squawk broke Reggie's thoughts.

OOOHHHHH! WOWWWWW!

'Come and check out this view, Reggie!' Pipsquark squealed from the living room.

Reggie followed Pipsquark's voice to the huge bay window of the apartment and he had to admit he was blown away. He could see all the way down to the ocean, where lights twinkled on the water.

'It's quite something, isn't it?' Kai said as Pipsquark took pictures of the sea.

As Kai headed to her room to get her pocket money the TV blared and Reggie and Pipsquark joined Kai's parents on their couch.

. . . NOT ONLY WILL THE ROOF NEED TO BE REBUILT IN PARTS DUE TO PREVIOUS SHODDY REPAIRS, BUT PROGRESS ON THE TOWN HALL HAS NOW BEEN INDEFINITELY DELAYED AS A THEFT IN THE MAYOR'S OFFICE IS BEING INVESTIGATED.

THE ARCHITECTS' MODELS HAVE BEEN STOLEN, AND NOW THEY NEED TO BE REMADE. THE TOWN HALL, THE APARTMENTS WITH THE TEENY-TINY SOFAS . . . THEY PINCHED THE LOT!

NG NEWS | BREAKING NEWS | BREA

'Let's go!' Kai announced, waving her purse at Reggie and Pipsquark. She wanted to use the pocket money she'd saved to buy them some chips from the market.

Reggie and Pipsquark said goodbye to Kai's parents and followed Kai out.

As Pipsquark ran on ahead to take photos, Kai strode alongside Reggie.

Reggie side-eyed the seagull, not quite sure how to fill the silence. But he needn't have worried. Kai took on the role of tour guide and gave him a full history of Seagull Rock.

'. . . It's actually not one cave but a series of caves that make up the apartment block,' Kai said. 'All the seagull nests have been hollowed out of the stone.' She tapped the wall. 'Us seagulls have been here for hundreds of years. There's a fascinating chapter on the architecture of Seagull Rock in *The History of Bearburgh* by O.L.D. Grizzly if you want to know more.'

'Great,' was about all Reggie could muster up.

Why did Kai have to know everything and be so perfect? But his reply only seemed to encourage her.

'There are deeper caves at the base of the rock,' she said, linking a wing through Reggie's arm. 'That's where smugglers and pirates used to hide their treasures.'

Reggie was relieved when, a moment later, they were hit by the hustle and bustle of the market and a squeal from Pipsquark, who insisted on the trio having a selfie by the busy stalls.

There were hundreds of stands packed into the huge cave. Seagull traders squawked loudly over one another about their wares. Reggie was jostled left and right as shoppers pushed past. The air was stuffy with the smell of fish and chips, and Reggie felt a rush of excitement as he eyed the colourful vegetables, trinkets, and antiques that lined the narrow walkways.

'Can you believe this place?' Pipsquark shouted over the chaos. Her eyes were wide with excitement. There were more folk in that one cave alone than in the whole of Little Critter.

'Have a look, have a look,' a chip stall owner squawked at Reggie. 'It's a pound a pottle or five for six.'

The stall owner was speaking so fast, Reggie could barely make out what he was saying.

'Poundapottle, poundapottle, poundapottle,' the

seagull repeated.

'We'll take one,' Kai said, stepping up confidently.

She grabbed a heaped carton of chips and handed over her money to the stall owner.

'These are the second-best chips in Seagull Rock,' she said, offering them around. 'They have the perfect balance of salt and vinegar.'

As they left the busy market and headed towards the harbour, Reggie gobbled up the delicious hot chips and reached for another pawful.

Among the row of shops, there was one that was boarded up with a 'Closed Down' sign. Reggie recognized the logo above the door.

'Is that the fish and chip shop from the news?' he asked.

'Yes,' Kai said sadly. 'Also, it's my go-to place for the

first-best chips in Seagull Rock.'

Then she shook her head. 'Or at least it was,'
she corrected.

Reggie saw that outside the shop were cards and flags
full of support for the shop owner.

The three kneeled down to look at all the messages.

'No one in Seagull Rock believes Mr Gabbiano is a criminal,' Kai said, bitterly.

'It's rare that a criminal isn't actually a criminal,' Reggie said, trying not to point out the obvious.

'He didn't do it,' Kai snapped. 'Mr Gabbiano is one of the kindest seagulls Seagull Rock has ever known. He's the reason our home is protected.' She waved her wings at the scene around them. 'If he hadn't fought for us to stay living here, my grandparents would have been forced out of their cave so developers could turn it into a car park.'

Kai scrunched up the empty chip packet into an angry tight ball and lobbed it into the nearby bin. 'Some fox, who has never lived here in his life, turned up and suddenly declared Mr Gabbiano a criminal after a shoddy five-minute investigation.'

Reggie squared up to Kai. 'Detective Fox is a brilliant detective,' he retorted. 'And if he can detect a criminal in five minutes that's because he's incredible.'

'You don't know anything about it!' Kai shouted back. 'You have no idea about seagulls. Mr Gabbiano would never sell out-of-date chips because we actually know how to look after our own.'

And with that, Kai stalked off back to her apartment block leaving a shocked Reggie and Pipsquark in her wake.

Pipsquark sighed and turned to Reggie.

'I know you think Detective Fox is perfect. And I get that he's your hero,' she said quietly. 'But I remember how he brushed us off the first time we met him.'

Her eyes were sad and her shoulders drooped as she crossed her wings.

Then she followed Kai through the caves, leaving Reggie all alone.

CHAPTER FIVE

Reggie tossed onto his side in his sleeping bag. Left. Then right. Then a whole turn of a circle back onto his left again. The apartment was silent except for the gentle snores coming from Kai's parents' room. And the rustling of Reggie in his sleeping bag.

He peered over at Pipsquark who was tucked in beside Kai. Both were fast asleep.

Reggie remembered Granny Lavender once saying

that it was hard for a guilty conscience to sleep. He shifted about in his sleeping bag again at the thought. He didn't have a guilty conscience. Not really. He did feel bad that he'd upset Kai. But he had to defend Detective Fox. What else was he meant to do? In fact, if anyone should feel guilty and be wide awake in the middle of the night, it should be Pipsquark who had said absolutely nothing to stand up for the detective.

No. Reggie didn't have a guilty conscience at all. It was just that he wasn't used to sleeping on a cliff floor.

He sat up in the dark and looked out at the huge view of the sea. What had been dazzling before with its wide blue, gently dotted with streaks of white, now looked dark and menacing in the moonlight. The waves looked like ghosts charging across the surface and diving into the deep.

A shiver ran up his spine and shuddered the sleeping bag off his shoulders. He grabbed the edges, pulling it back up around his neck.

'It's just a bit of moonlight,' he reassured himself. 'It's just the sound of waves.' He almost laughed out loud at the silliness of it all, and he shook his head for being such a jittery bunny. 'There's no such thing as ghosts,' he reminded himself.

He plumped up his pillow and slid back down into his sleeping bag. As he lay back, he yawned loudly and felt his eyelids grow heavy.

But that was when he heard the sound.

He sat bolt upright again. The fur on his back was standing on end.

OOoooooOOoooO!

The lights flickered across the horseshoe bay of Seagull Rock and then DARKNESS!

'AHHHHHHHHHHHH!' Reggie screamed.

'Reggie?' Pipsquark screamed back.

'Pipsquark?' Kai screamed too.

'WHAT'S HAPPENING?' Reggie shrieked, unable to keep the shrill terror out of his voice.

His legs felt shaky, and his heart was beating so fast he thought his chest might explode.

'It's OK, it's OK,' Kai whimpered. 'This is what always happens during the hauntings.'

It might've been what always happened but Reggie could hear Kai was scared.

And though he didn't want to admit it, he was too.

A glow fell across the room as Kai's mum and dad hurried in holding torches. As the room lit up, Reggie could see Pipsquark cowering next to Kai, both with faces as ashen as the ghost Reggie thought he had just heard.

'Did you hear that, Dad?' Kai said, her voice small and quivering. 'I heard a howl.'

'I did too,' her dad replied, cuddling her. 'But you're safe here.'

'Are you OK?' Kai's mum asked, sitting down by Reggie.

'I'm fine,' Reggie feigned. 'It's just so dark.'

Kai's parents looked out at the sea. Every single light in Seagull Rock was still out.

'Right, kids,' Kai's dad said, straightening up. 'We're going out to investigate with the Seagull Patrol—'

'But Dad,' Kai interrupted.

'You'll be fine,' Kai's dad reassured her. 'It's safe in the apartment. But stay put until we come home, OK?'

'You mustn't leave unless you absolutely have to,' Kai's mum added. 'Dad and I will leave our torches but I'm sure the lights will be back on in no time.'

As Kai's parents left the apartment, Reggie could hear squawks and muffled chatter as the Seagull Patrol gathered on each floor.

'We should go and investigate,' Pipsquark announced as soon it was just the three of them in the room.

She shook off her sleeping bag and grabbed a torch.

'Wait,' Kai yelped. 'We're meant to stay here.'

Reggie couldn't believe he was about to agree with

Kai but she was right. That ghostly howl still rang in his ears. He wasn't keen to go out into the pitch-black night anytime soon.

'I think Kai's right,' Reggie said.

'No,' Pipsquark said, sticking out her beak. 'We promised we would not go out unless we absolutely had to. And I think we absolutely must investigate what is going on.'

'But . . . the ghost?' Kai faltered.

Pipsquark sat down next to her friend. 'We all heard something. And we all saw the lights go out. But we don't know it's a ghost because we don't have any proof.'

'If it's not a ghost then what is it?' Reggie said.

'I don't know,' Pipsquark admitted. 'But we need to find out. We're detectives, Reggie. We hunt for clues and find answers. That's our job.' Pipsquark straightened up and turned to Kai. 'If anyone can get to the bottom of this, it's us.'

Pipsquark's words rang true and the trembling feeling in Reggie's gut stopped. She was right. Nancy had told them to always follow the evidence and right now there was no evidence that a ghost was haunting Seagull Rock. But there was also no evidence that it wasn't.

IT WAS TIME FOR REGGIE RABBIT, DETECTIVE AND HIS FEARLESS PARTNER PIPSQUARK TO FIND OUT THE TRUTH.

THEY HEADED OUT INTO
THE NIGHT . . .

DUCKING BEHIND BIG
BIN BAGS . . .

AND HIDING BEHIND
LAMP POSTS . . .

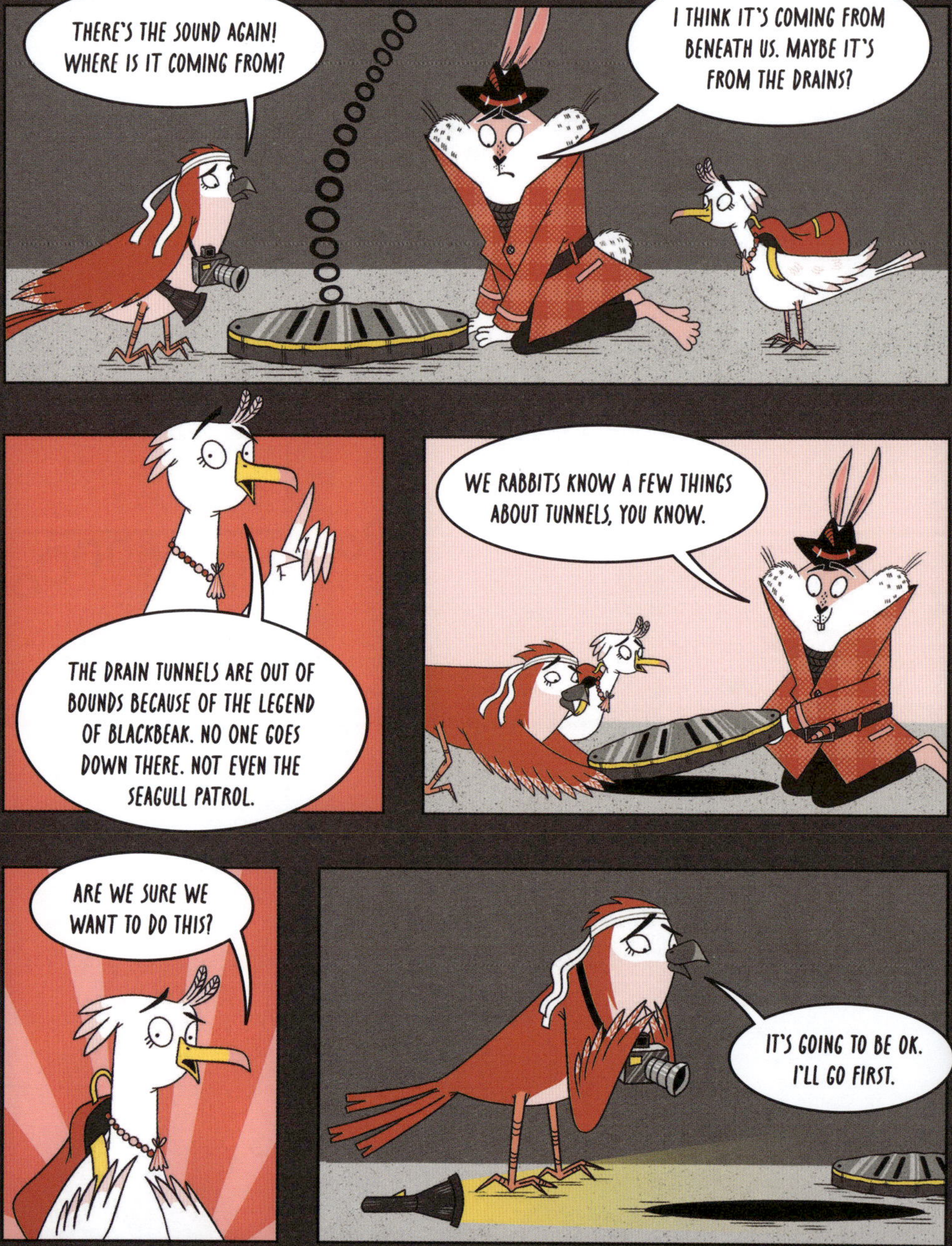
THERE'S THE SOUND AGAIN! WHERE IS IT COMING FROM?
I THINK IT'S COMING FROM BENEATH US. MAYBE IT'S FROM THE DRAINS?
THE DRAIN TUNNELS ARE OUT OF BOUNDS BECAUSE OF THE LEGEND OF BLACKBEAK. NO ONE GOES DOWN THERE. NOT EVEN THE SEAGULL PATROL.
WE RABBITS KNOW A FEW THINGS ABOUT TUNNELS, YOU KNOW.
ARE WE SURE WE WANT TO DO THIS?
IT'S GOING TO BE OK. I'LL GO FIRST.

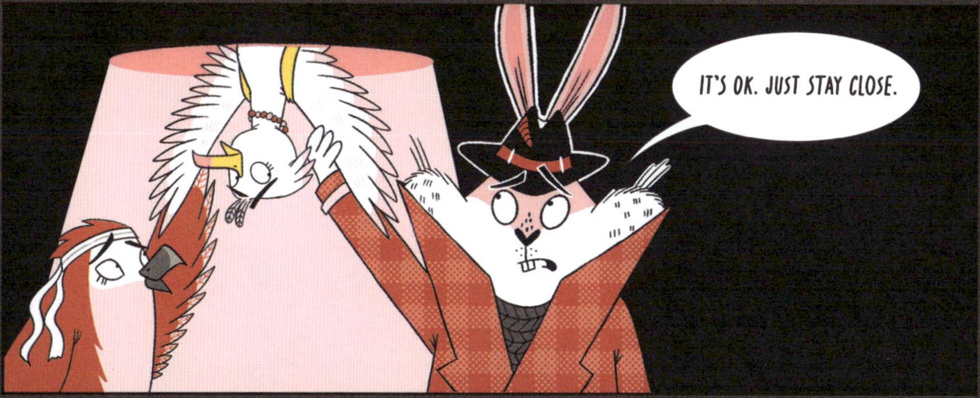
IT'S OK. JUST STAY CLOSE.

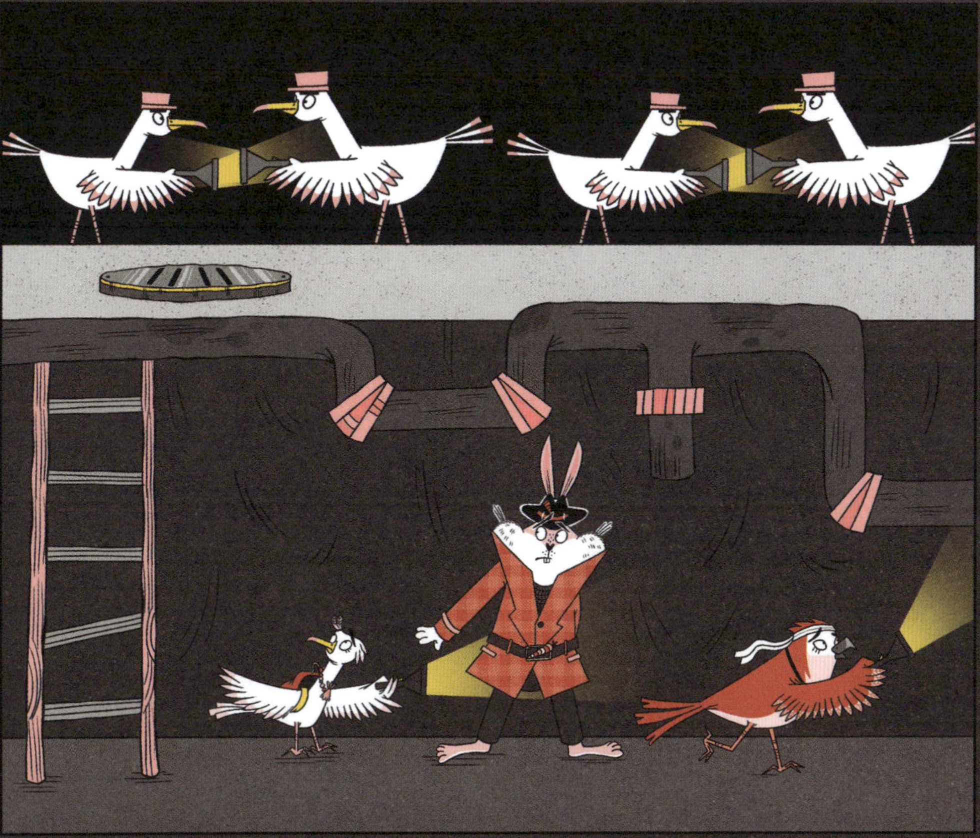

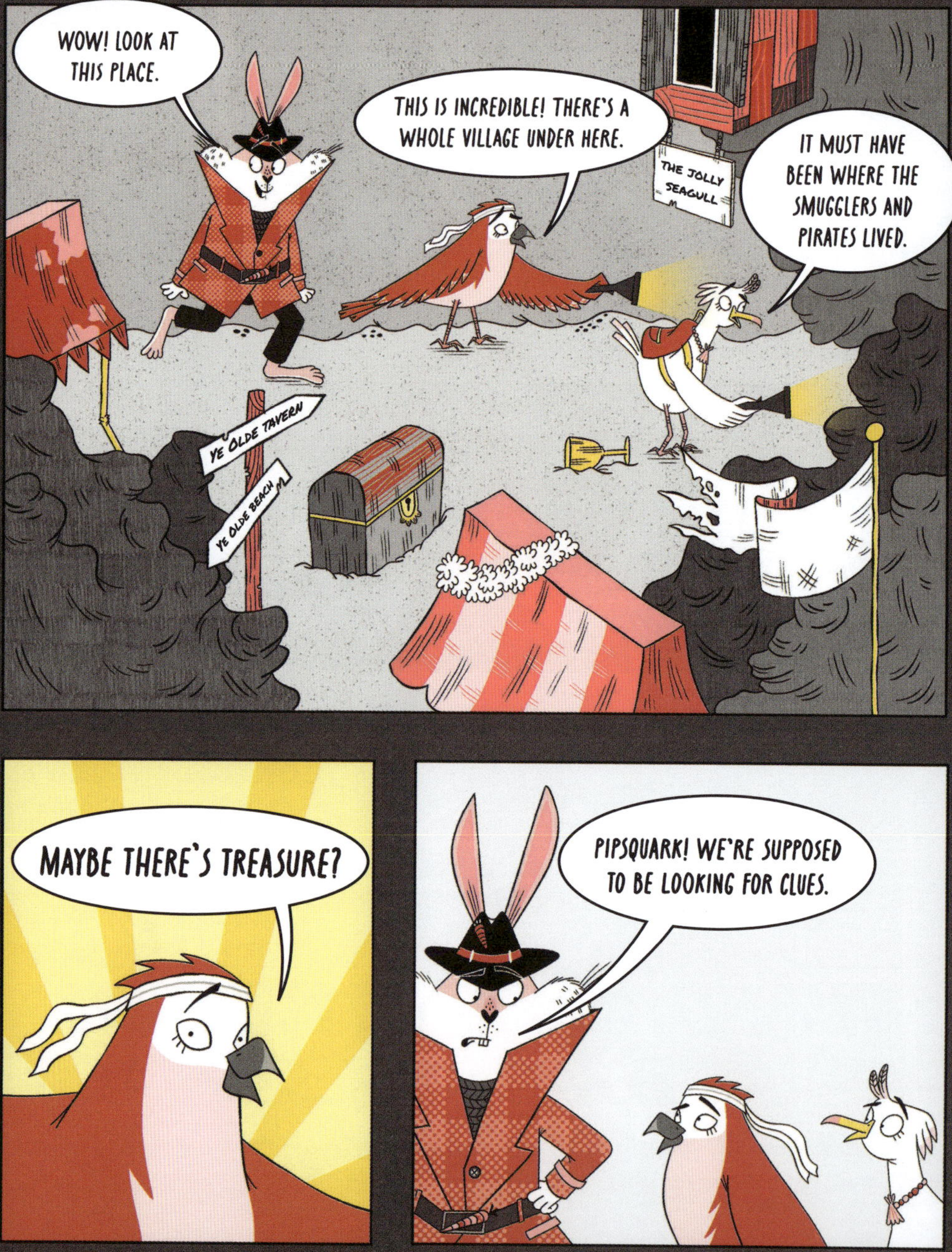
WOW! LOOK AT THIS PLACE.
THIS IS INCREDIBLE! THERE'S A WHOLE VILLAGE UNDER HERE.
THE JOLLY SEAGULL
IT MUST HAVE BEEN WHERE THE SMUGGLERS AND PIRATES LIVED.
YE OLDE TAVERN
YE OLDE BEACH
MAYBE THERE'S TREASURE?
PIPSQUARK! WE'RE SUPPOSED TO BE LOOKING FOR CLUES.

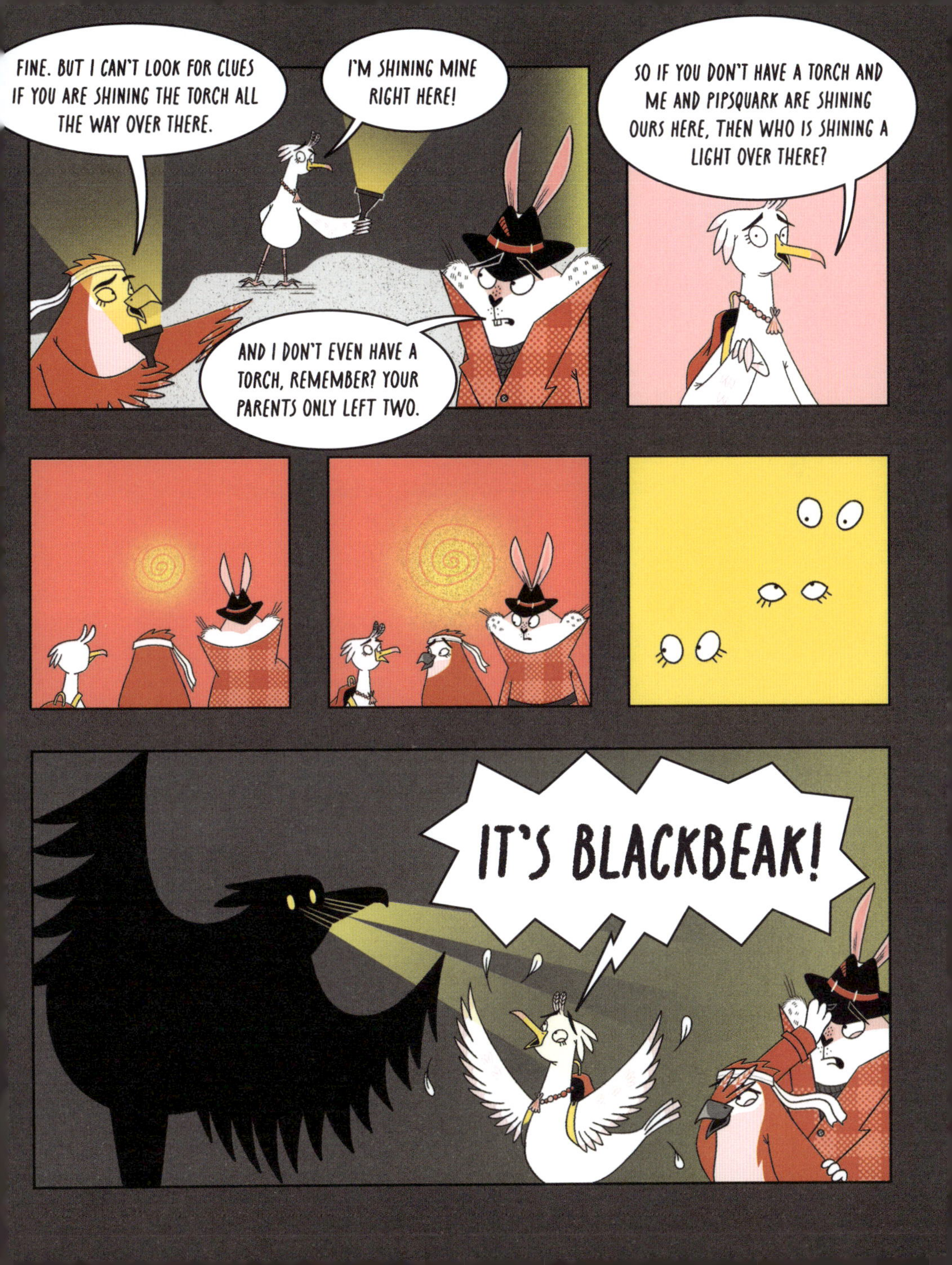
FINE. BUT I CAN'T LOOK FOR CLUES IF YOU ARE SHINING THE TORCH ALL THE WAY OVER THERE.
I'M SHINING MINE RIGHT HERE!
AND I DON'T EVEN HAVE A TORCH, REMEMBER? YOUR PARENTS ONLY LEFT TWO.
SO IF YOU DON'T HAVE A TORCH AND ME AND PIPSQUARK ARE SHINING OURS HERE, THEN WHO IS SHINING A LIGHT OVER THERE?
IT'S BLACKBEAK!

CHAPTER SIX

Reggie, Pipsquark, and Kai didn't sleep that night. They were all thankful to hear Kai's parents return to the apartment not long after they had raced home from the tunnels and huddled together in a frightened ball in their sleeping bags.

At breakfast Kai shot Reggie a relieved look as Pipsquark managed to keep the conversation flowing with Kai's mum and dad. The last thing the trio needed was an interrogation about why they were all so tired, especially as, as far as Kai's parents knew, they were sleeping safely in the apartment and absolutely not on a ghost hunt in the old smugglers' tunnels. Knowing that both he and Kai were thinking the same thing, Reggie wondered if he had been too quick to judge the seagull. A guilty twinge in his tummy made it impossible for him to finish the final bit of his cereal.

'Why did the lights go out?' Pipsquark asked, interrupting Reggie's thoughts.

Kai's mum and dad exchanged an awkward glance.

'I suppose Kai has told you about the ghost haunting Seagull Rock?'

Reggie nodded along with Pipsquark.

'Well, it looks like the ghost damaged the wiring around the town, among other things,' Kai's dad said, wiping the weariness from his face with a long swipe of his wing. 'It's going to be quite a while until the electricity is up and running.'

'So, no TV?' Kai exclaimed.

'No TV, I'm afraid.' Kai's mum winced. 'And I was hoping to watch the seagull-diving championships today!'

The rattle of the letter box made Reggie, Kai, and Pipsquark jump out of their seats.

'You all seem a bit on edge this morning,' Kai's mum commented as she went to retrieve the post. 'Is everything OK?'

'We're fine, Mum,' Kai said quickly. 'It's just the shock of not having TV.'

Kai's mum came back to the kitchen with a glossy flyer.

'It's a new development on the other side of the city,' Kai's mum said, quickly scanning the advertisement.

'Apartment swaps available for residents of Seagull Rock?' Kai's dad read off the cover. 'That sounds good!'

'You're right,' Kai's mum agreed. 'Maybe this rock is just getting too old.' She flicked the kitchen light switch on and off to prove the point. The bulb didn't turn on. It didn't flicker. There wasn't even so much as a quiet hum.

'Don't say that!' Kai spoke up, her voice prickly. 'I love our home and I don't ever want us to leave.'

An uncomfortable silence fell over the table and Reggie took that as a cue to tidy away his breakfast bowl.

'Maybe we can go out for the day?' he suggested and was glad when Kai's parents agreed. They ushered the trio out, even offering to do the washing up, which was normally Kai's chore at home. They must have been feeling as awkward as Reggie at Kai's reaction to the flyer.

As soon as they were outside, Reggie slipped on his trench coat and hat. The air fizzed with the saltiness of the sea, and the sun warmed his long ears.

Reggie saw Kai's mood lift as soon as he'd spoken.

It was short bus ride to the city. Reggie, Pipsquark, and Kai set themselves up in the back corner of the bus, away from the other passengers, including a gull chick who was trying to flick everyone that passed with the sticky juice dripping from her ice lolly.

'Pipsquark,' Reggie started, once they were in their seats. His voice was low so both Pipsquark and Kai had to lean in to hear him. 'Last night you said we needed

evidence. Well two strange things have happened in Seagull Rock recently—'

'That's right,' Kai agreed. 'First Mr Gabbiano was arrested for something he would never have done, and second the ghost of Blackbeak appeared.'

She shuddered as she remembered the previous night.

'Exactly,' Reggie said. 'But we don't have any evidence to connect the two. It could just be a coincidence.'

'But we also don't have any evidence to not connect the two,' Pipsquark piped up.

Reggie nodded. 'That's why I think we need to see Detective Fox.'

Kai grunted. She didn't seem keen on the idea and after their argument Reggie knew she would need some convincing.

'If I'm willing to believe you about Mr Gabbiano,' Reggie offered, 'would you be willing to take a chance on Detective Fox for me?'

He held out his paw and watched as Kai stared at it for a moment before grabbing it and shaking it hard.

'Deal,' she said and while Pipsquark grinned to see her two best friends getting on, Reggie was sure he spotted the tiniest of smiles on Kai's face too.

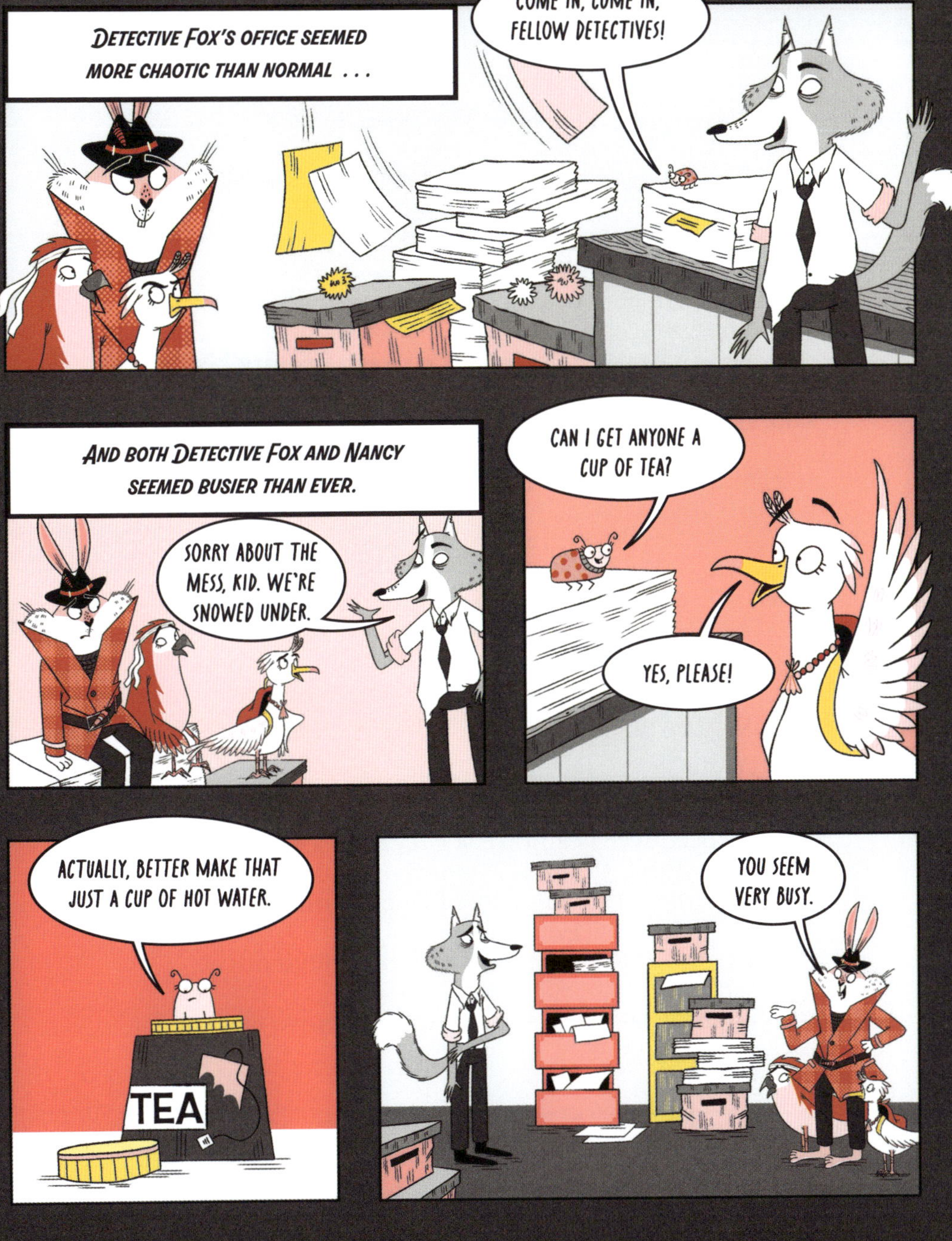
DETECTIVE FOX'S OFFICE SEEMED MORE CHAOTIC THAN NORMAL . . .
COME IN, COME IN, FELLOW DETECTIVES!
AND BOTH DETECTIVE FOX AND NANCY SEEMED BUSIER THAN EVER.
SORRY ABOUT THE MESS, KID. WE'RE SNOWED UNDER.
CAN I GET ANYONE A CUP OF TEA?
YES, PLEASE!
ACTUALLY, BETTER MAKE THAT JUST A CUP OF HOT WATER.
TEA
YOU SEEM VERY BUSY.

'We're busy,' Detective Fox started. 'But . . .'

He stopped and sighed and looked over at Nancy who returned his harried gaze.

'. . . we're being rushed off our feet with petty cases that Mayor Bear is demanding take top priority,' Nancy said, finishing Detective Fox's sentence. 'It's part of her "clean up the worst and put Bearburgh first" campaign. She knows small cases are quicker to solve and if we solve twice as many small cases in the time it takes to do one big case, she can tell the people of Bearburgh she's done twice the work of cutting crime. It's all about the numbers.'

'All cases are important, of course,' the detective said. 'But it's been weeks and weeks of chasing small cases when we know there must be bigger crimes happening.'

He waved at the window which, though dusty and caught with cobwebs, had an impressive view of downtown Bearburgh.

Nancy held up a file at the group. 'Look at this!' she laughed frustratedly. 'Someone left litter in the park! The park warden was happy to clear it up but the mayor wants us to investigate immediately. And that's on top of solving the Case of the Missing Model Buildings from the mayor's office.' She tossed the folder onto a pile of files that were holding open the kitchenette door. 'It's hardly the Great Carrot Heist, is it?'

Case of the
Discarded
Litter

IS THAT WHAT YOU CALL MR GABBIANO'S ARREST? A SMALL CASE? HE DIDN'T DESERVE TO BE ARRESTED. HE WOULD NEVER HAVE DONE SOMETHING LIKE THAT.

I'M SORRY, KID. OUR JOB IS TO FOLLOW THE EVIDENCE. IT LED US STRAIGHT TO HIS FISH AND CHIP SHOP AND WE DISCOVERED A FRY-TENING AMOUNT OF EVIDENCE IN HIS BACK ROOM.

YOU DON'T KNOW WHAT YOU ARE TALKING ABOUT! MR GABBIANO IS THE KINDEST SEAGULL—

OOPS, I LEFT MY BACKPACK OPEN.

WHY DO YOU HAVE ALL THESE?

THEY'VE BEEN ARRIVING IN THE LETTER BOX FOR THE LAST WEEK OR SO. I'VE BEEN TAKING THEM SO MOTHER AND FATHER DON'T SEE THEM. WITH EVERYTHING GOING ON AT SEAGULL ROCK, I'M WORRIED THEY WILL WANT US TO MOVE. IT WAS ALL POINTLESS ANYWAY—THEY SAW ONE THIS MORNING.

There was the Case of the Cats Disturbing the Peace by Singing at Midnight . . .

And there was the Case of the Bears Licking Honey Straight Out of the Jars in the Supermarket . . .

And the Case of Ravens Loitering at the Top of High Buildings and Dropping Rotten Bananas off the Roof Edges . . .

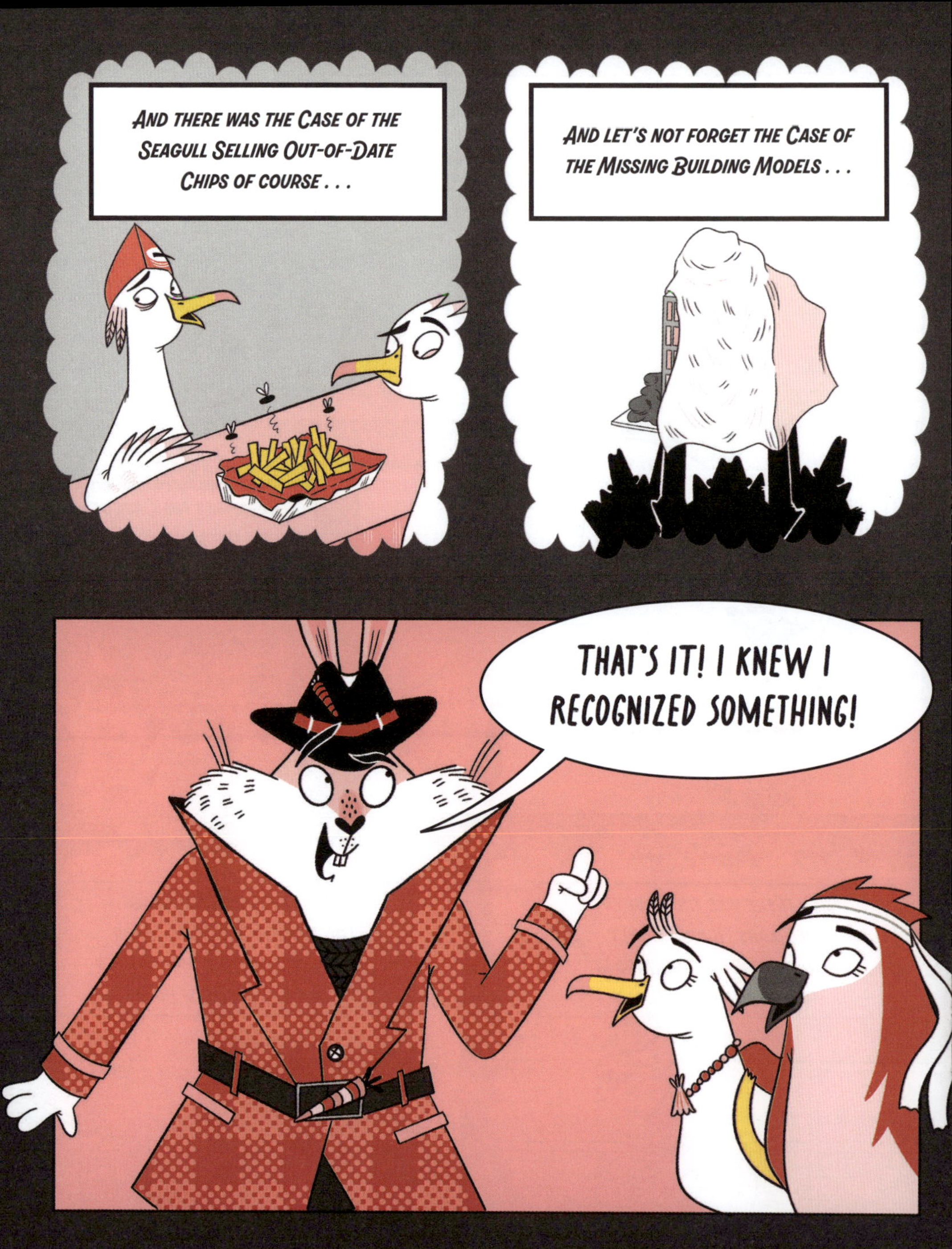
AND THERE WAS THE CASE OF THE SEAGULL SELLING OUT-OF-DATE CHIPS OF COURSE . . .
AND LET'S NOT FORGET THE CASE OF THE MISSING BUILDING MODELS . . .
THAT'S IT! I KNEW I RECOGNIZED SOMETHING!

CHAPTER SEVEN

LATER, IN MASQUE TOWER . . .

OUT OF MY WAY, YOU LAZY RAVENS!

Nora's amazing business plan

SHOO! YOU'RE INTERRUPTING MY PRESENTATION!

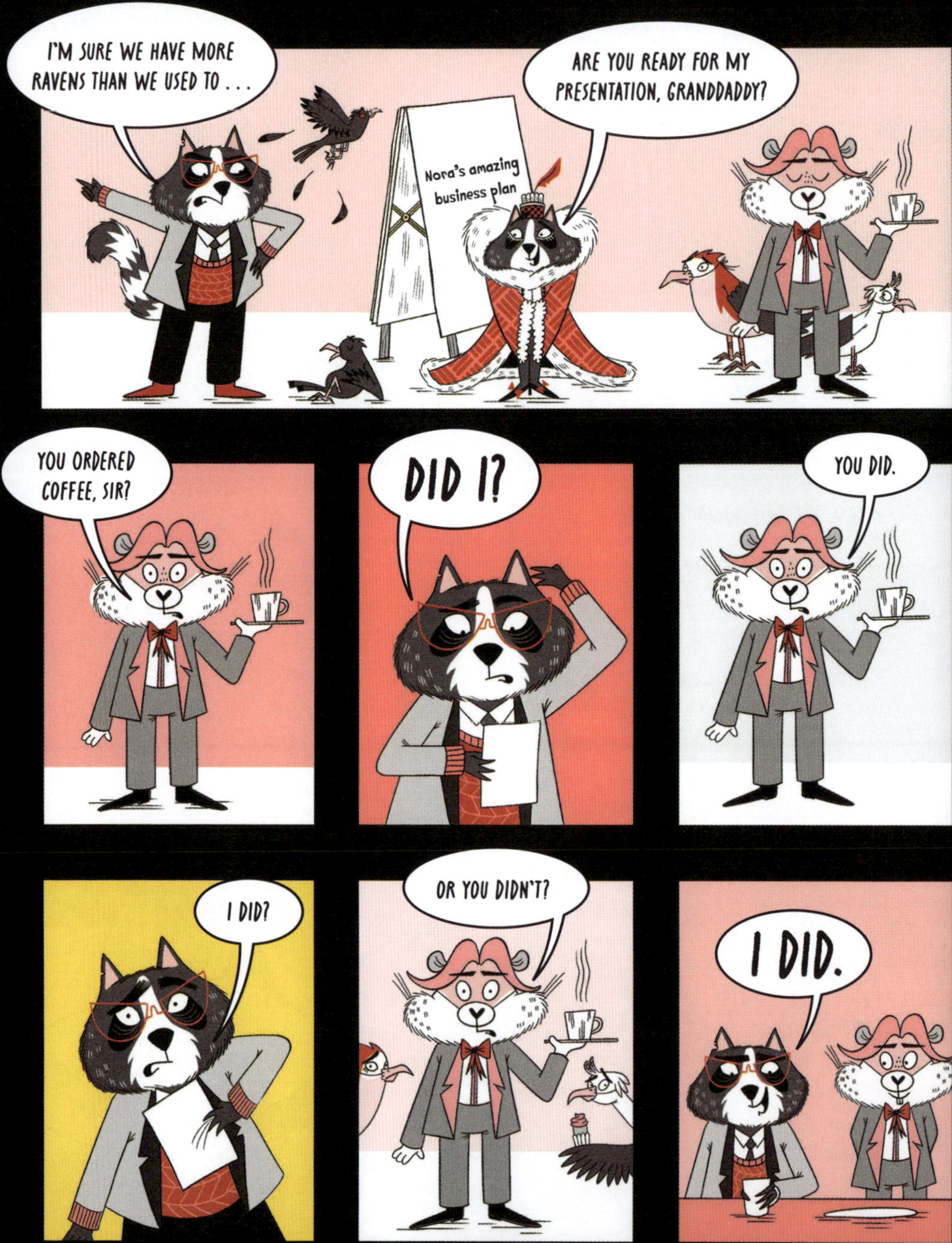
I'M SURE WE HAVE MORE RAVENS THAN WE USED TO . . .
Nora's amazing business plan
ARE YOU READY FOR MY PRESENTATION, GRANDDADDY?
YOU ORDERED COFFEE, SIR?
DID I?
YOU DID.
I DID?
OR YOU DIDN'T?
I DID.

HOLY RACCOONS. THIS IS HOTTER THAN THE SUN!

DO YOU HAVE ANY COLD WATER?

GAH! NORA! I CAN'T EVEN AFFORD DECENT STAFF BECAUSE OF YOU. I SHOULD SEND YOU STRAIGHT TO RINGTAIL MANOR, SCHOOL FOR WAYWARD RACOONS, RIGHT NOW.

Nora's amazing business plan

YOU WON'T WANT TO DO THAT JUST YET, GRANDDADDY. IT'S TIME FOR THE NEXT STAGE OF MY PLAN AND I'M ABOUT TO MAKE YOU A FORTUNE.

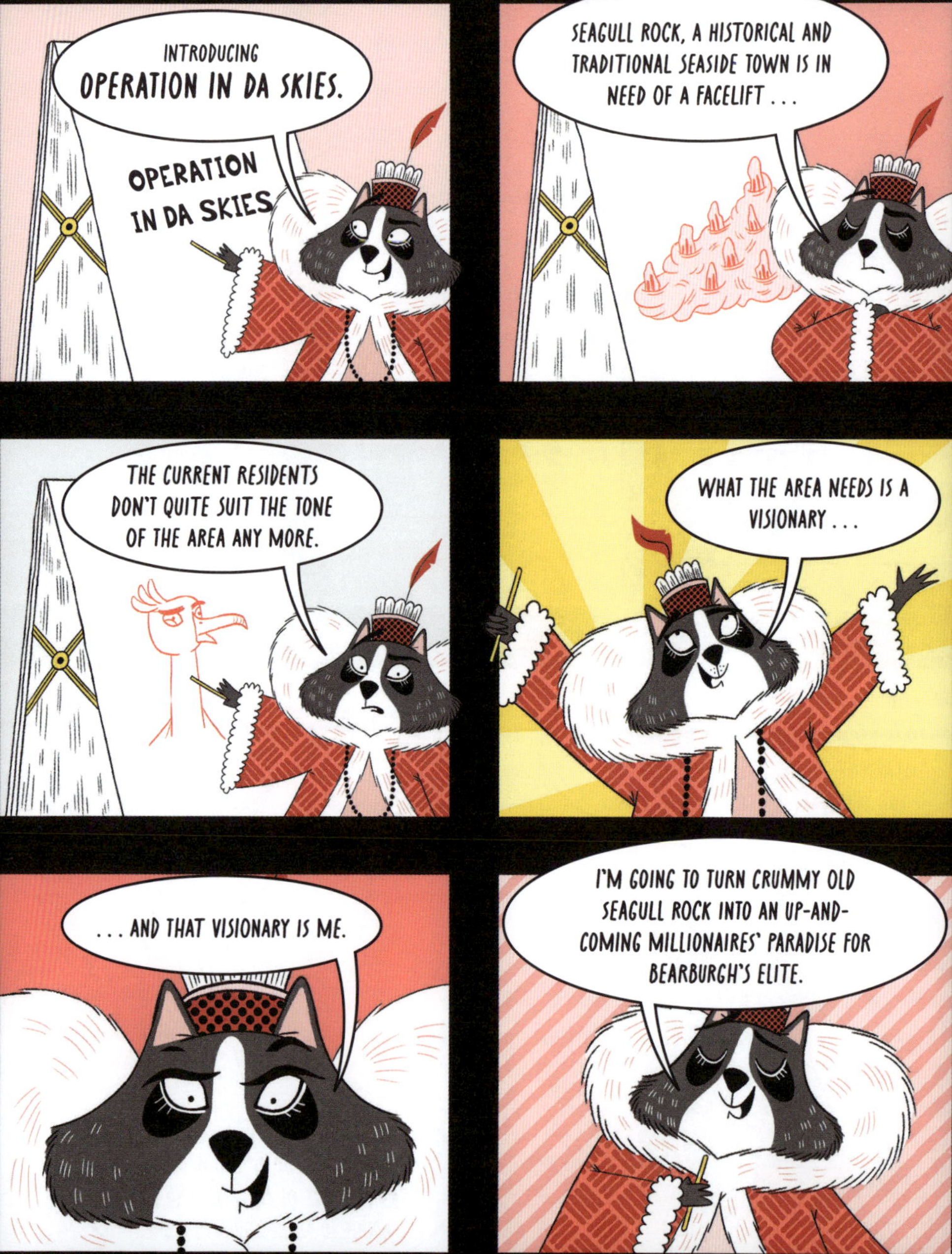
INTRODUCING OPERATION IN DA SKIES.
OPERATION IN DA SKIES
SEAGULL ROCK, A HISTORICAL AND TRADITIONAL SEASIDE TOWN IS IN NEED OF A FACELIFT . . .
THE CURRENT RESIDENTS DON'T QUITE SUIT THE TONE OF THE AREA ANY MORE.
WHAT THE AREA NEEDS IS A VISIONARY . . .
. . . AND THAT VISIONARY IS ME.
I'M GOING TO TURN CRUMMY OLD SEAGULL ROCK INTO AN UP-AND-COMING MILLIONAIRES' PARADISE FOR BEARBURGH'S ELITE.

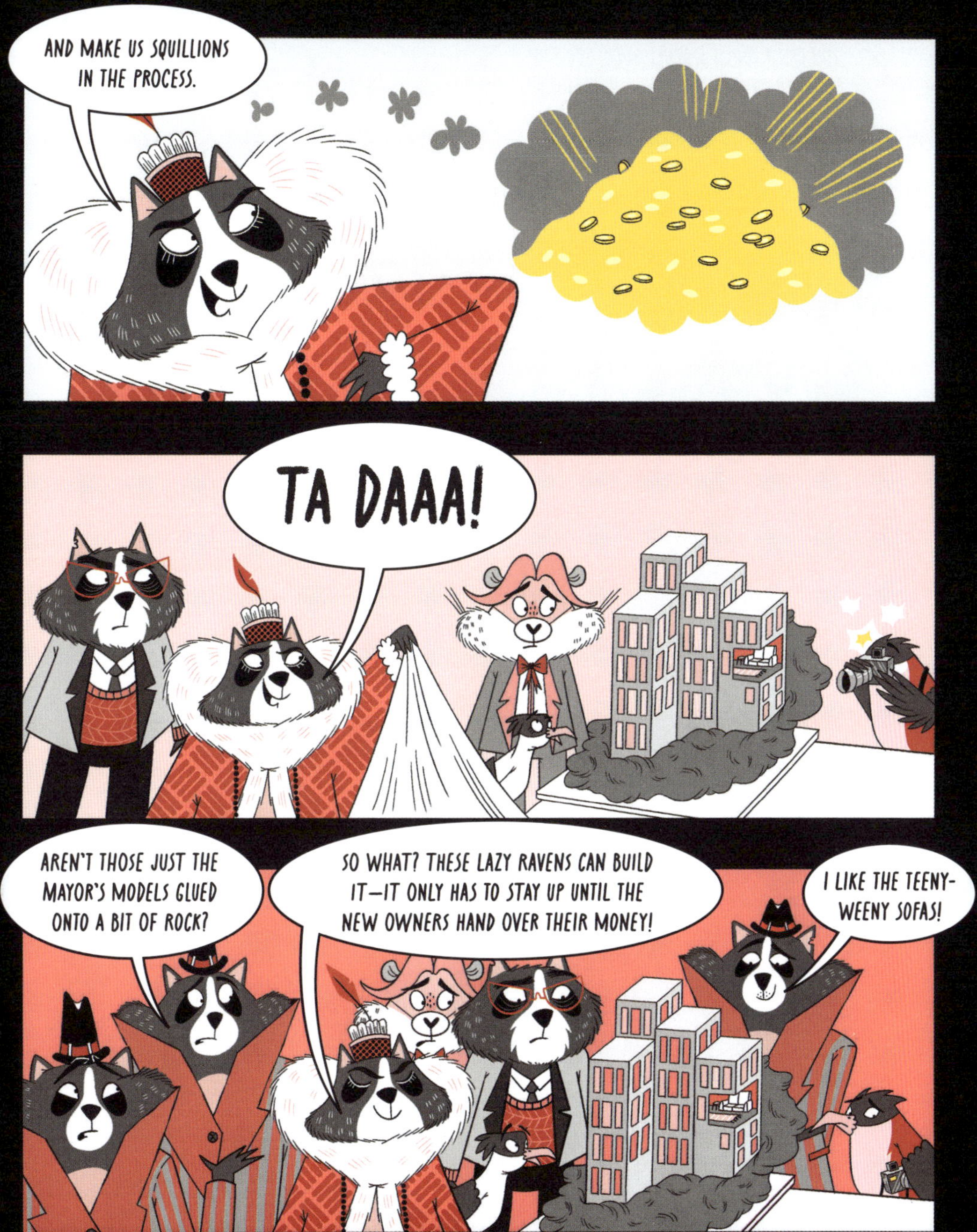
AND MAKE US SQUILLIONS IN THE PROCESS.
TA DAAA!
AREN'T THOSE JUST THE MAYOR'S MODELS GLUED ONTO A BIT OF ROCK?
SO WHAT? THESE LAZY RAVENS CAN BUILD IT—IT ONLY HAS TO STAY UP UNTIL THE NEW OWNERS HAND OVER THEIR MONEY!
I LIKE THE TEENY-WEENY SOFAS!

YOU CAN'T TOUCH SEAGULL ROCK, YOU FOOL. IT'S AN AGREEMENT THAT THE MAYOR'S OFFICE MADE BACK IN THE DAY WITH SOME WRETCHED, TROUBLE-MAKING ACTIVISTS. NOW, IT'S THE LAW. IF YOU WANT TO BUILD ON SEAGULL ROCK THE SEAGULLS HAVE TO AGREE TO LEAVE THEMSELVES.

AND WHY WOULD THEY DO THAT?

OH, BUT I'VE THOUGHT OF THAT ALREADY, GRANDDADDY.

I'M WORKING ON SOMETHING THAT IS GOING TO HAVE THOSE SEAGULLS RUNNING FAR, FAR AWAY FROM THEIR PRECIOUS SEAGULL ROCK, NEVER TO RETURN.

HE HUH EGH HGH HE.

NO, MORE LIKE MU-HWA-HA-HA

CHAPTER EIGHT

'Pipsquark, how come your sleeping bag is on my side?' Kai teased.

'It's only a little over,' Pipsquark protested.

Reggie laughed as he dug his paw into the huge bowl of popcorn for another mouthful and watched his friends jostle for prime space on the floor in front of the TV.

'We have the Little Critter Vegetable Fair coming up soon,' Reggie said as Pipsquark and Kai talked about when they would next have a sleepover. 'Everyone can stay at mine if you want?'

'Are you sure?' Kai asked, excitedly.

'Of course!' Reggie replied. 'Though you'll have to put up with Lettice's snoring again.'

The trio of friends broke into fits of giggles at the reminder of Lettice and her nightly sounds.

'You're all in a good mood,' Kai's mum said, coming in to join the group. 'I hope you get a good sleep tonight without any spooky noises.'

Kai stiffened at the mention of the ghost and her mum threw a wing around her and cuddled her close.

'Even if we hear the ghost tonight, you are not to worry, OK?' Kai's mum continued. 'It will hopefully be one of the last times we'll hear Blackbeak.'

'Really?' Kai said.

Kai's mum squeezed Kai's shoulders. 'Well, your father and I were thinking it might be an idea to move somewhere completely ghost-free soon.'

Everyone watched Kai carefully, knowing how she felt about moving away.

'We had a virtual tour of a new flat at Ocean Retreat,' Kai's mum said gently to Kai. 'It was so nice, love. There was plenty of space for you to have a big room and even more space for your friends to sleep over.'

She peered at Kai and stroked the feathers on her head. 'We'll show you the virtual tour tomorrow if you want? It's so great that we don't need to travel all the way there to see our new flat. You can go on the tour as many times as you like and plan your whole room.'

There was a moment of silence as everyone waited to see how Kai would respond.

'That sounds great, Mum,' Kai replied. 'I'd really like that.'

If Kai's mum was surprised, she didn't mention it. Instead, she beamed at her daughter with delight and gave her a big hug. Reggie, Pipsquark, and Kai said goodnight to the grown-ups.

As the snores from Kai's parent's room started to fill the apartment, Reggie put on his detective hat.

'Tonight, we solve the mystery of the Ghost of Seagull Rock!'

WITH KAI'S PARENTS FAST ASLEEP, THE TRIO SNUCK OUT INTO THE NIGHT . . .

OOOOoooOooooOOO!

LET'S GO.

WHA . . . WHA . . . WHAT IS THAT?

I THINK IT'S THE GHOST OF BLACKBEAK.

ooOOo!

I'M SO SCARED, PIPSQUARK. WHAT IF THE GHOST GETS ME?!

I'M SCARED TOO. I'M NOT READY TO BE A GHOSTLY PARAKEET ON THE SHOULDER OF A GHOSTLY PIRATE.

oOOOoooooOOo!

I'M SO GLAD THE SEAGULLS ARE LEAVING SEAGULL ROCK. THIS GHOST IS FAR TOO SCARY FOR US.

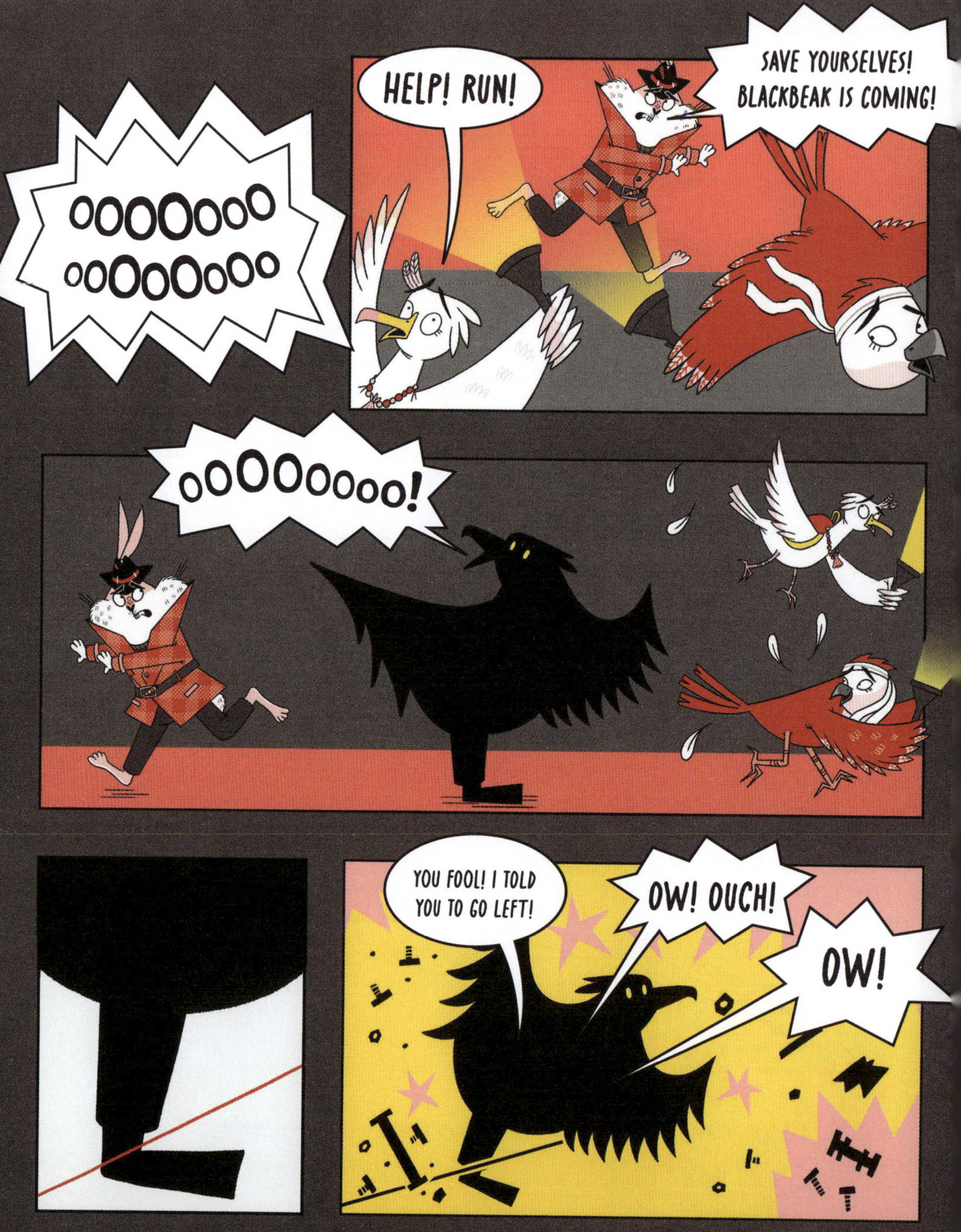
OOOOOOO
OOOOOOOOO
HELP! RUN!
SAVE YOURSELVES! BLACKBEAK IS COMING!
OOOOOOOO!
YOU FOOL! I TOLD YOU TO GO LEFT!
OW! OUCH!
OW!

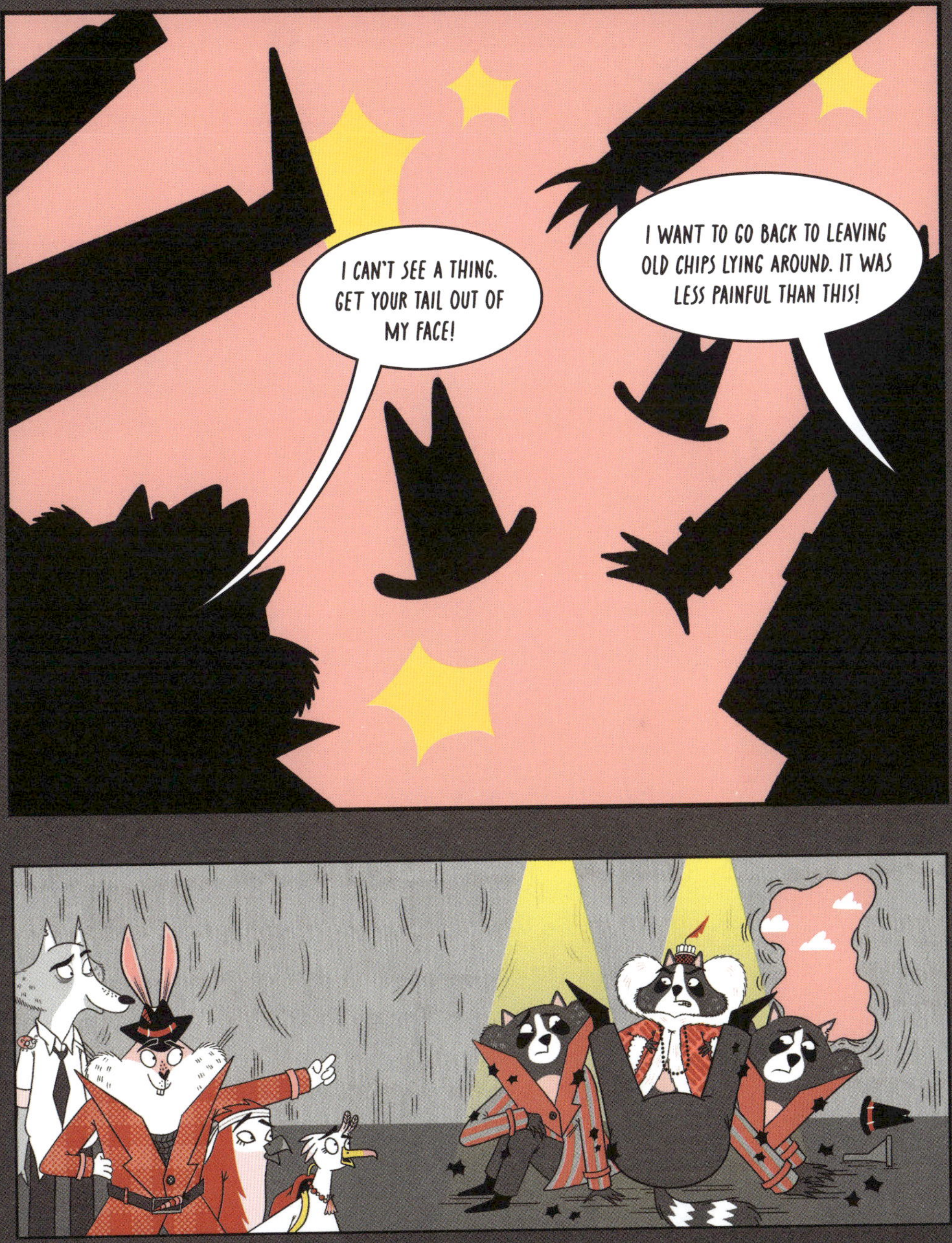
I CAN'T SEE A THING. GET YOUR TAIL OUT OF MY FACE!
I WANT TO GO BACK TO LEAVING OLD CHIPS LYING AROUND. IT WAS LESS PAINFUL THAN THIS!

CHAPTER NINE

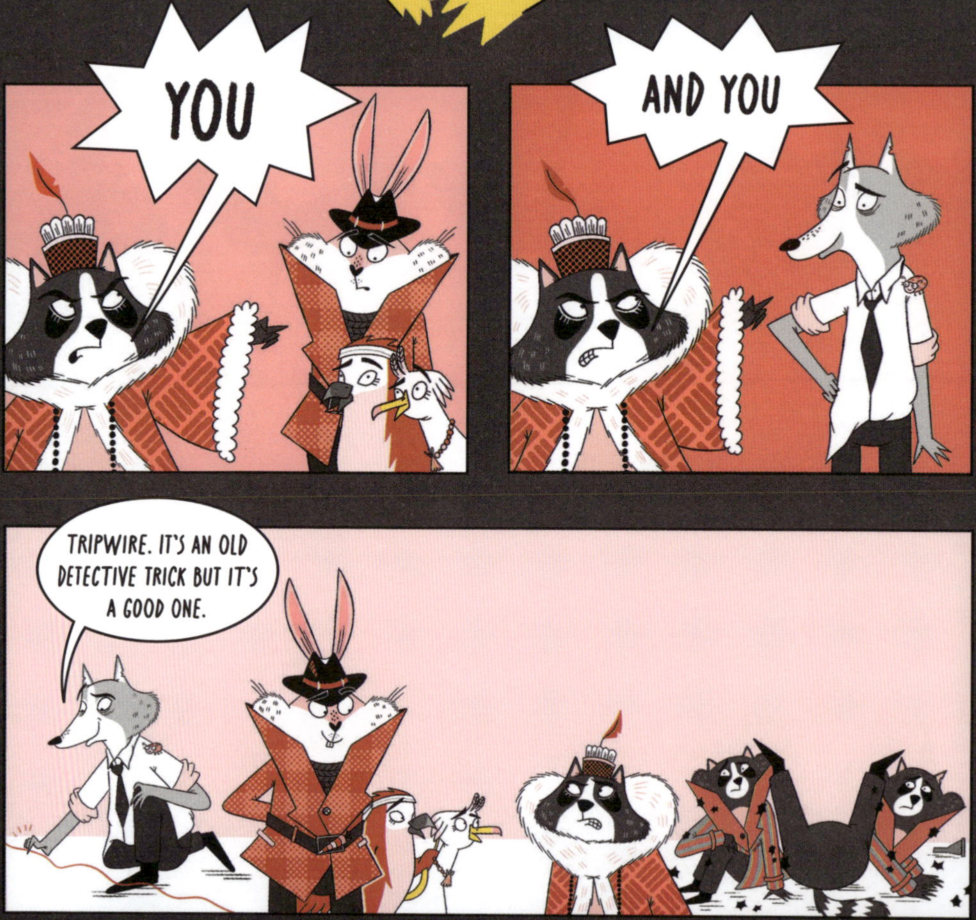
YOU
AND YOU
TRIPWIRE. IT'S AN OLD DETECTIVE TRICK BUT IT'S A GOOD ONE.

HOW DID YOU KNOW?

THIS IS THE KIDS' CASE SO I THINK THEY SHOULD EXPLAIN.

YOU NEARLY HAD ME, MASQUE.

I DIDN'T BELIEVE KAI AND HER GHOST STORY WHEN I FIRST MET HER . . .

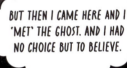

BUT THEN I CAME HERE AND I 'MET' THE GHOST. AND I HAD NO CHOICE BUT TO BELIEVE.

BUT PIPSQUARK ALWAYS SAYS THAT A DETECTIVE NEEDS TO TRUST THEIR INSTINCTS.

I HAD A GNAWING FEELING ABOUT MR GABBIANO I COULDN'T SHAKE. KAI WAS SURE HE WOULD NEVER COMMIT A CRIME, NO MATTER HOW PETTY.

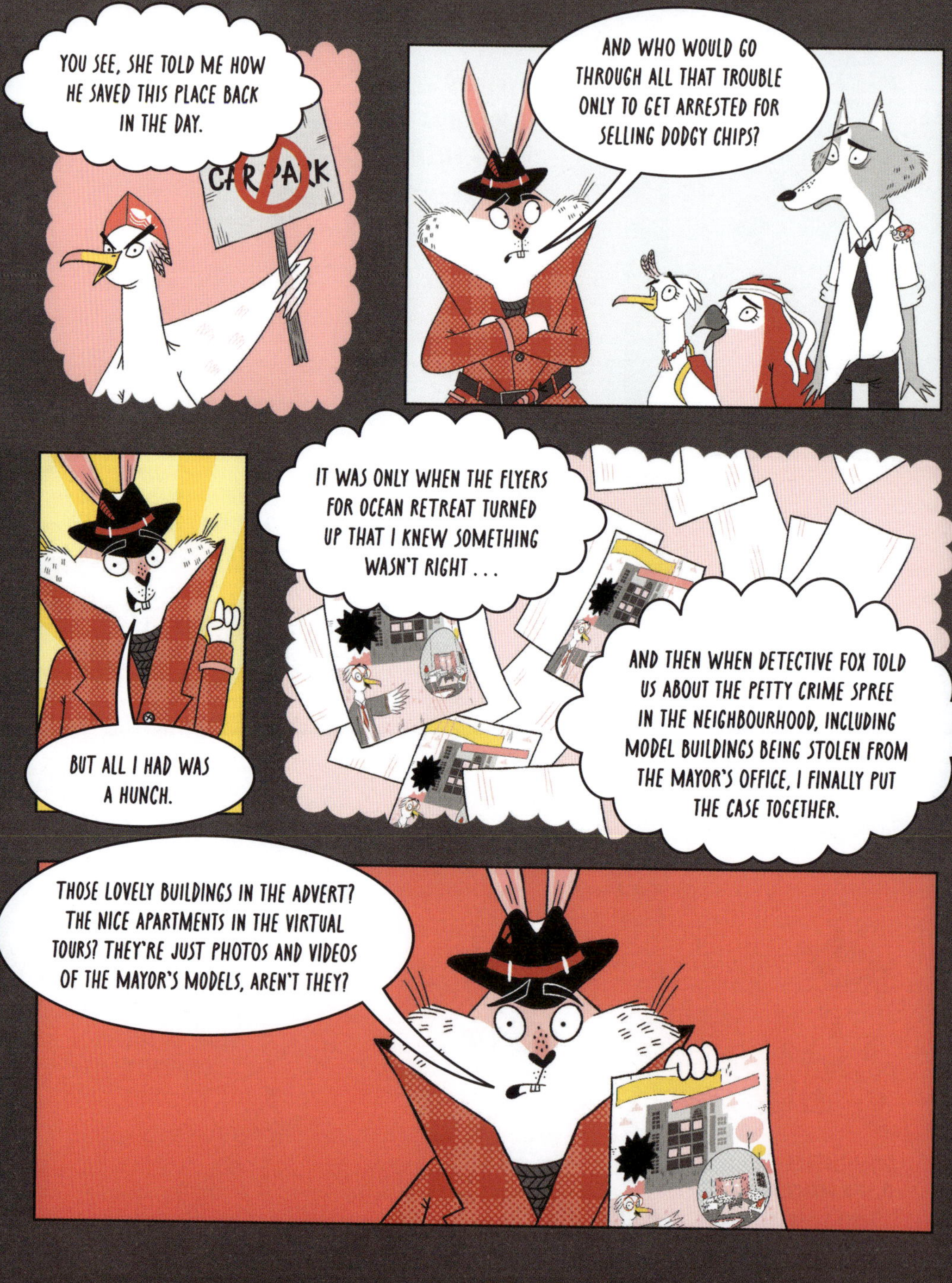
YOU SEE, SHE TOLD ME HOW HE SAVED THIS PLACE BACK IN THE DAY.
CAR PARK
AND WHO WOULD GO THROUGH ALL THAT TROUBLE ONLY TO GET ARRESTED FOR SELLING DODGY CHIPS?
BUT ALL I HAD WAS A HUNCH.
IT WAS ONLY WHEN THE FLYERS FOR OCEAN RETREAT TURNED UP THAT I KNEW SOMETHING WASN'T RIGHT . . .
AND THEN WHEN DETECTIVE FOX TOLD US ABOUT THE PETTY CRIME SPREE IN THE NEIGHBOURHOOD, INCLUDING MODEL BUILDINGS BEING STOLEN FROM THE MAYOR'S OFFICE, I FINALLY PUT THE CASE TOGETHER.
THOSE LOVELY BUILDINGS IN THE ADVERT? THE NICE APARTMENTS IN THE VIRTUAL TOURS? THEY'RE JUST PHOTOS AND VIDEOS OF THE MAYOR'S MODELS, AREN'T THEY?

THIS CASE STANK OF THE MASQUES BUT GOOD DETECTIVES ALWAYS FOLLOW THE EVIDENCE.

WE HEARD ON TV THAT BEAVER BUILDERS WERE REBUILDING THE TOWN HALL THAT THE MASQUES HAD ORIGINALLY BUILT.

WE KNEW YOU WOULDN'T BE HAPPY ABOUT A HUGE PROJECT GOING TO SOMEONE ELSE. AND THEN THE MAYOR LAUNCHED A BIG CRACKDOWN ON CRIME. THAT MUST HAVE MADE YOU VERY ANGRY . . .

YOU HAD A REASON TO SABOTAGE THE BUILD. YOU HAD A REASON TO STEAL THE MODELS FROM THE MAYOR'S OFFICE.

SO, WE WENT TO MASQUE TOWER.

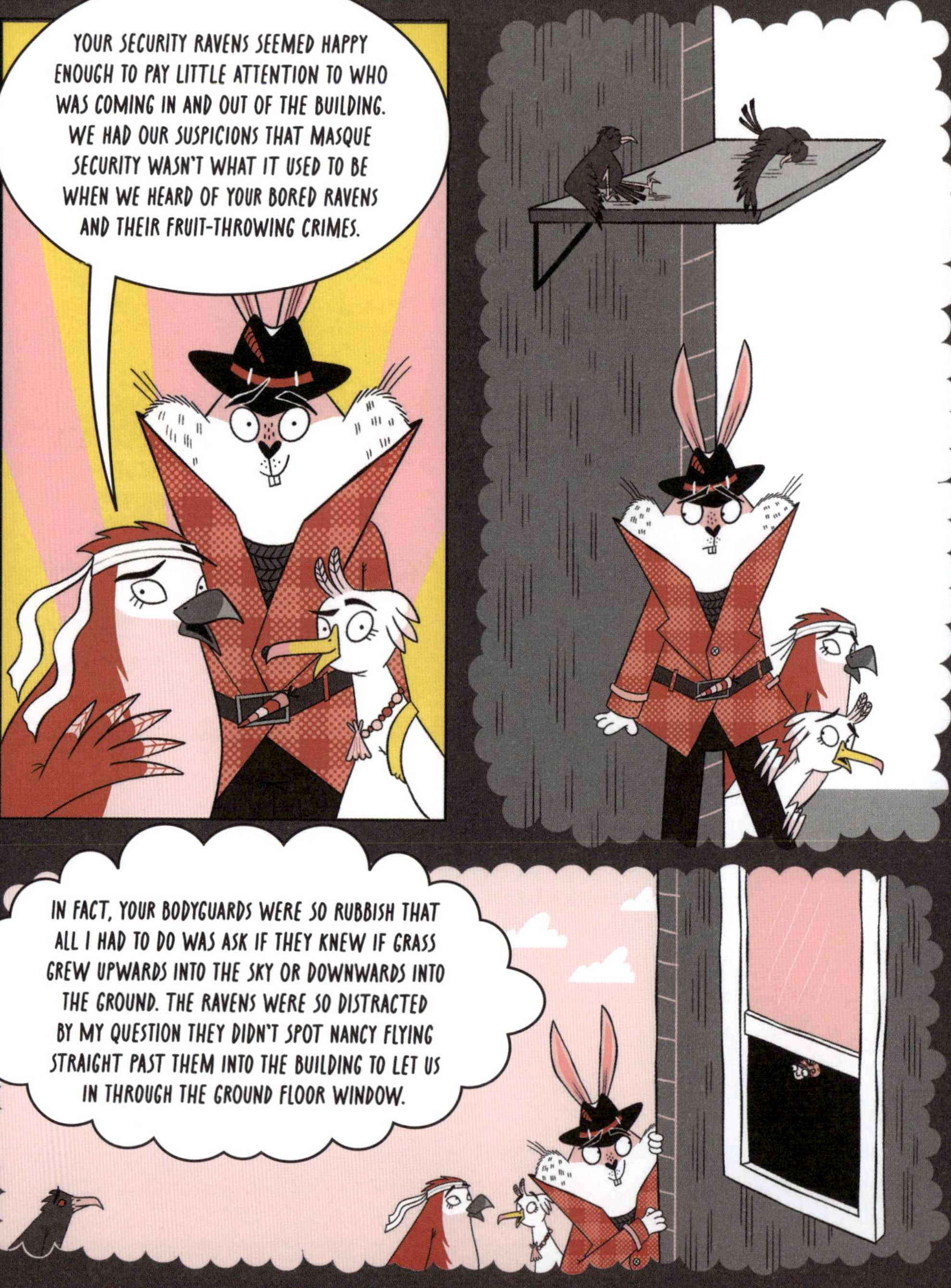
YOUR SECURITY RAVENS SEEMED HAPPY ENOUGH TO PAY LITTLE ATTENTION TO WHO WAS COMING IN AND OUT OF THE BUILDING. WE HAD OUR SUSPICIONS THAT MASQUE SECURITY WASN'T WHAT IT USED TO BE WHEN WE HEARD OF YOUR BORED RAVENS AND THEIR FRUIT-THROWING CRIMES.
IN FACT, YOUR BODYGUARDS WERE SO RUBBISH THAT ALL I HAD TO DO WAS ASK IF THEY KNEW IF GRASS GREW UPWARDS INTO THE SKY OR DOWNWARDS INTO THE GROUND. THE RAVENS WERE SO DISTRACTED BY MY QUESTION THEY DIDN'T SPOT NANCY FLYING STRAIGHT PAST THEM INTO THE BUILDING TO LET US IN THROUGH THE GROUND FLOOR WINDOW.

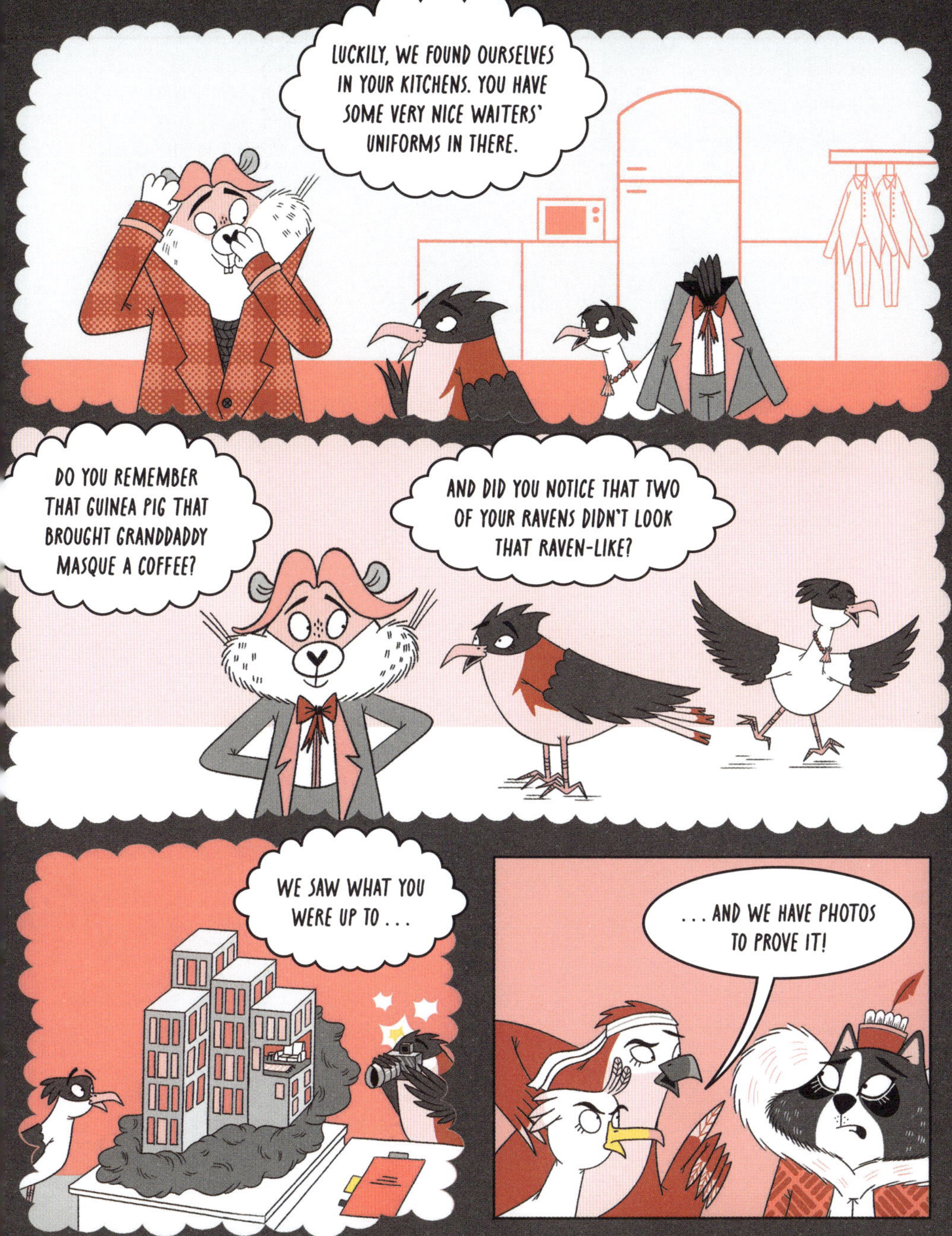
LUCKILY, WE FOUND OURSELVES IN YOUR KITCHENS. YOU HAVE SOME VERY NICE WAITERS' UNIFORMS IN THERE.
DO YOU REMEMBER THAT GUINEA PIG THAT BROUGHT GRANDDADDY MASQUE A COFFEE?
AND DID YOU NOTICE THAT TWO OF YOUR RAVENS DIDN'T LOOK THAT RAVEN-LIKE?
WE SAW WHAT YOU WERE UP TO . . .
. . . AND WE HAVE PHOTOS TO PROVE IT!

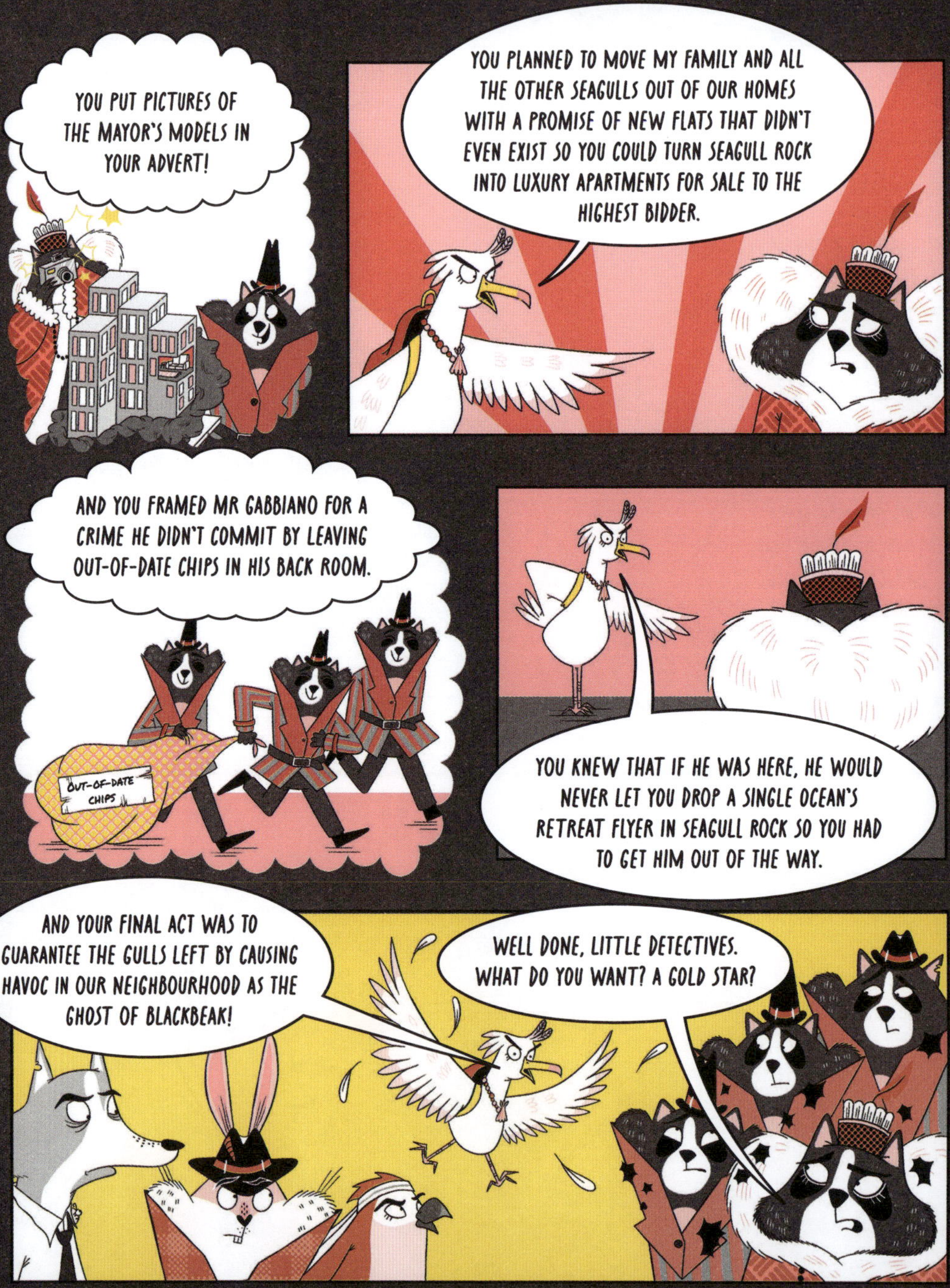
YOU PUT PICTURES OF THE MAYOR'S MODELS IN YOUR ADVERT!
YOU PLANNED TO MOVE MY FAMILY AND ALL THE OTHER SEAGULLS OUT OF OUR HOMES WITH A PROMISE OF NEW FLATS THAT DIDN'T EVEN EXIST SO YOU COULD TURN SEAGULL ROCK INTO LUXURY APARTMENTS FOR SALE TO THE HIGHEST BIDDER.
AND YOU FRAMED MR GABBIANO FOR A CRIME HE DIDN'T COMMIT BY LEAVING OUT-OF-DATE CHIPS IN HIS BACK ROOM.
OUT-OF-DATE CHIPS
YOU KNEW THAT IF HE WAS HERE, HE WOULD NEVER LET YOU DROP A SINGLE OCEAN'S RETREAT FLYER IN SEAGULL ROCK SO YOU HAD TO GET HIM OUT OF THE WAY.
AND YOUR FINAL ACT WAS TO GUARANTEE THE GULLS LEFT BY CAUSING HAVOC IN OUR NEIGHBOURHOOD AS THE GHOST OF BLACKBEAK!
WELL DONE, LITTLE DETECTIVES. WHAT DO YOU WANT? A GOLD STAR?

'The police are on the way,' Nancy said. 'Your life of crime is over.'

Nora stood and shook off the last bits of her Blackbeak costume as her brothers still fumbled through hooks and thread, trying to untie themselves. She delicately stepped over the tripwire and held out her wrists.

'So, arrest me then,' she suggested.

'Stay right where you are, Nora Masque,' Detective Fox warned.

Nora sidled back towards a small gap in the wall where a sliver of moonlight shone in. Fox took a step towards her, but Kai held out her wing.

'She's just bluffing. She can't escape that way,' Kai said. 'There's a thirty-metre drop out there.'

Nora cocked her head and smiled evilly at Kai.

'You've forgotten one thing,' she said. 'Masques always plan for the worst-case scenario.'

She glanced over at her brothers and smirked. 'I knew if we were caught, us Masques couldn't escape,' she said. 'Well, at least not all of us.'

'Rocco, Ricci, Ronnie,' she called to her brothers, who were finally free of their Blackbeak costume. 'Your confessions for this entire crime are pinned inside your jacket pockets.'

As the brothers stood open-mouthed at Nora's announcement, Nancy patted them down and eventually fished out the confessions.

'She's right,' Nancy said, waving the notes in the air. 'They've each got a confession of their very own, admitting the whole crime.'

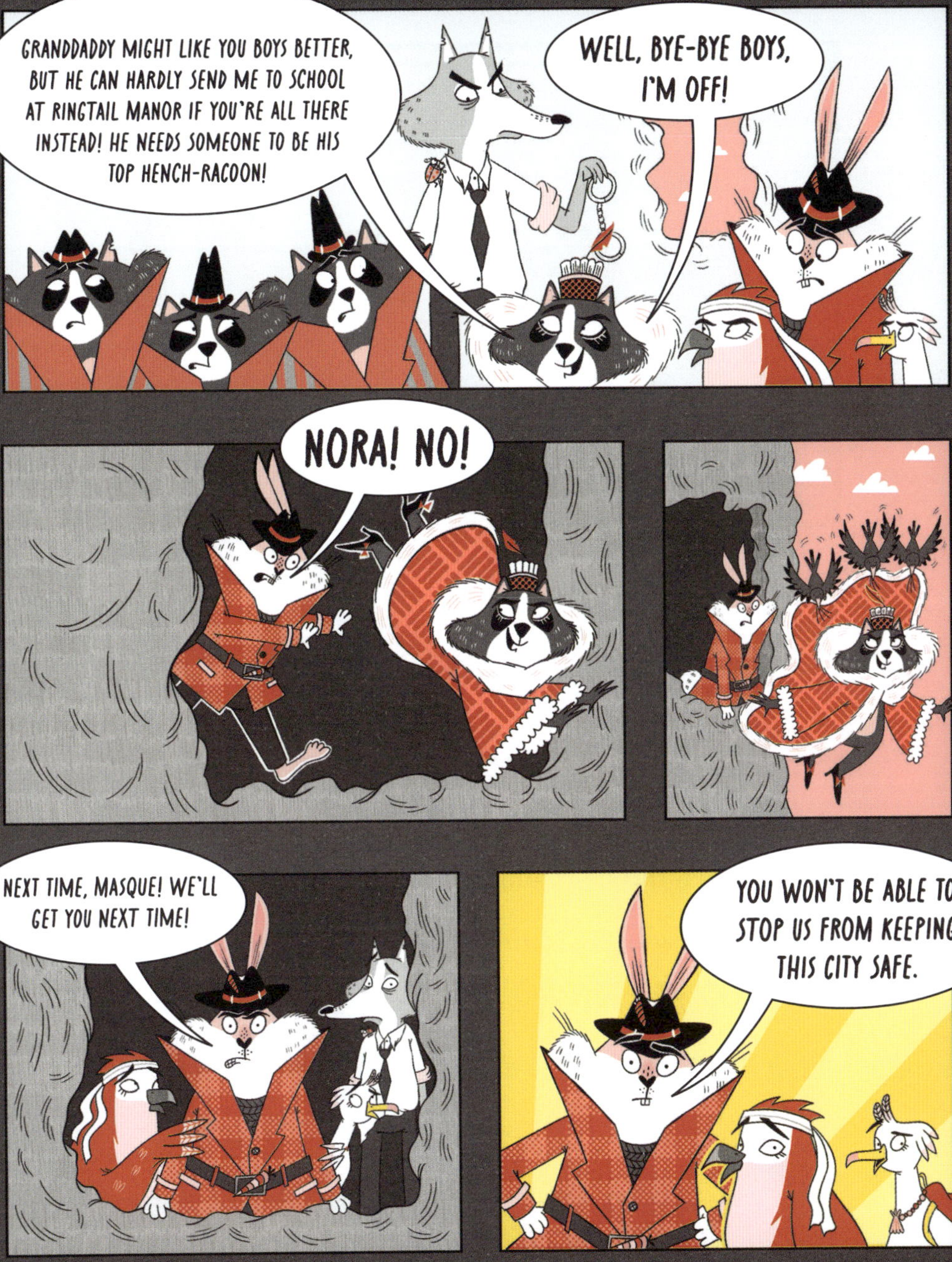
GRANDDADDY MIGHT LIKE YOU BOYS BETTER, BUT HE CAN HARDLY SEND ME TO SCHOOL AT RINGTAIL MANOR IF YOU'RE ALL THERE INSTEAD! HE NEEDS SOMEONE TO BE HIS TOP HENCH-RACOON!
WELL, BYE-BYE BOYS, I'M OFF!
NORA! NO!
NEXT TIME, MASQUE! WE'LL GET YOU NEXT TIME!
YOU WON'T BE ABLE TO STOP US FROM KEEPING THIS CITY SAFE.

EWS | BREAKING NEWS | BREAK

CHAPTER TEN

'Is Kai on yet?' Lettice asked, bounding into the Rabbit family's living room. She perched on the armrest of the couch next to Pipsquark and Reggie.

'Not yet,' Pipsquark said. 'It's the weather at the moment then the sport and then we are back to the Bearburgh headlines. I think Kai will be on then. Mum says the order on the news channel is always headlines, weather and sport on repeat so we are somewhere in the middle right now.'

'The weather looks good for the Vegetable Fair next weekend,' Granny Lavender said, sitting down next to Reggie on the sofa. She laid her knitting over his knees and started unravelling a ball of yarn. 'Is Kai joining us?'

'She is,' Pipsquark cheered before Reggie could say a word. 'It's her first Vegetable Fair, and she can't wait to see the Rabbits of Yesteryear exhibition!'

'Shhhh,' Lettice hushed. 'It's almost time for Kai's big moment.'

Reggie might have once had to use every last bit of self-control to keep from rolling his eyes at 'The Kai Show' but today he was excited to see his new friend on TV.

BONG! BONG!

The sound of the headlines rolling had Reggie's mum and dad running from the kitchen to the sofa.

The news presenter spoke for a moment about the Masque brothers before quickly handing over to Cattryn Catkin, who was on the scene at Seagull Rock.

'Extraordinary events at Seagull Rock last night have led to the arrest of the three grandsons of Mr Masque of Masque Industries,' she announced into her microphone. 'Mr Masque has denied all knowledge of the crimes and said that he will disown Rocco, Ricci, and Ronnie Masque with immediate effect.'

The screen filled with a clip of Granddaddy Masque outside Masque Tower. 'My granddaughter Nora is the future of Masque Industries now,' he said. And Reggie and Pipsquark exchanged glances as they saw Nora standing just behind her grandfather, grinning like it was the happiest day of her life.

Cattryn Catkin appeared on the screen again and spoke about how the Masque brothers had confessed to trying to acquire Seagull Rock through deception. She added that they had also admitted to framing Mr Gabbiano for a crime he didn't commit.

'That must be Mr Gabbiano,' Reggie said as a kind-looking, elderly seagull appeared on the TV.

'That is!' Granny Lavender said, looking up from her knitting.

'Do you know Mr Gabbiano?' Pipsquark asked.

'I do,' Granny Lavender said. 'I knew him from my youth. I joined his protests to save Seagull Rock from developers.'

This time it was Reggie's turn to hush the room.

'He's speaking,' Reggie said and all eyes were on the

TV again.

'Seagull Rock is safe again because of the heroic efforts of one small seagull who wanted to uncover the truth,' Mr Gabbiano said.

The camera panned to Kai who was smiling proudly at Mr Gabbiano.

The Rabbits' living room erupted into cheers as the camera stayed on Kai.

'. . . Seagull Rock is the oldest housing development in Bearburgh, though it is thought high-rise buildings have been around since the arrival of Roman seagulls, which could have been as early as 30 BCE.' Kai looked directly into the camera. 'That's over two thousand years ago which, by my estimation, is seven hundred and forty-nine thousand, eight hundred and forty-six days approximately . . .'

'You seem to know a lot about your home, Miss Kai,' interrupted Cattryn Catkin, looking very surprised.

Reggie giggled as the camera panned back to the news reporter.

'Kai does go on and on, doesn't she?' he ribbed Pipsquark.

'Look, I know some might find her annoying, but I like her,' Pipsquark said. 'You're annoying too sometimes, but I still like you.'

'Fair enough,' Reggie said, grinning at his friend.

As the rest of the Rabbit family chattered away about Kai's big TV moment, Pipsquark leaned in close and whispered, 'Do you feel like you should get some credit for solving this case? We would have had no idea about

Nora and her Blackbeak disguise if it wasn't for Reggie Rabbit, Detective.'

Reggie shook his head. 'It was ALL of us, Pipsquark. We are a detective team. But Kai deserves the limelight right now. No one loves Seagull Rock more than her, and besides, I think she quite likes being on TV.'

Kai was back on the screen receiving a certificate of bravery from Mayor Bear outside the partially refurbished town hall.

'Plus, Nora Masque is still out there, and I think she's far more dangerous than her granddaddy so it's probably best Reggie Rabbit, Detective and his partner Pipsquark keep a low profile for a while,' Reggie added, giving Pipsquark a nod.

As the news credits played out and the ads started before the next show, the Rabbit family made their way to the table for dinner.

Reggie laid out the cutlery as his dad piled the table with a huge steaming platter of vegetable casserole and dumplings.

Pipsquark helped herself as Lettice handed round the napkins.

'I still can't believe you and Pipsquark were fast asleep in bed while Kai solved the whole Mystery of the Ghost of Seagull Rock,' Granny Lavender said as she passed on a bowl of buttered parsnips to Reggie. She raised her eyebrows at Reggie, a knowing twinkle setting her brown eyes sparkling.

'I can't either,' Reggie agreed, giving her a wink.

MEET THE AUTHOR

Swapna Reddy

TOP
SECRET

Award-winning author Swapna Reddy, who also writes as Swapna Haddow, is the author of the Ballet Bunnies series. She lives in New Zealand with her husband and son and their dog, Archie. If she wasn't writing books, she would love to run a detective agency or wash windows because she's very nosy.

SECRET
FILES

Becka Moor

Becka Moor is an illustrator and designer who lives in Manchester with her fiancé and two cats, Hank and Martha. She has illustrated over 70 books (and counting!), including The Wigglesbottom Primary series. She enjoys watching cartoons, collecting mugs, critiquing baking shows, and leaving half-consumed beverages everywhere she goes.

STAY OUT

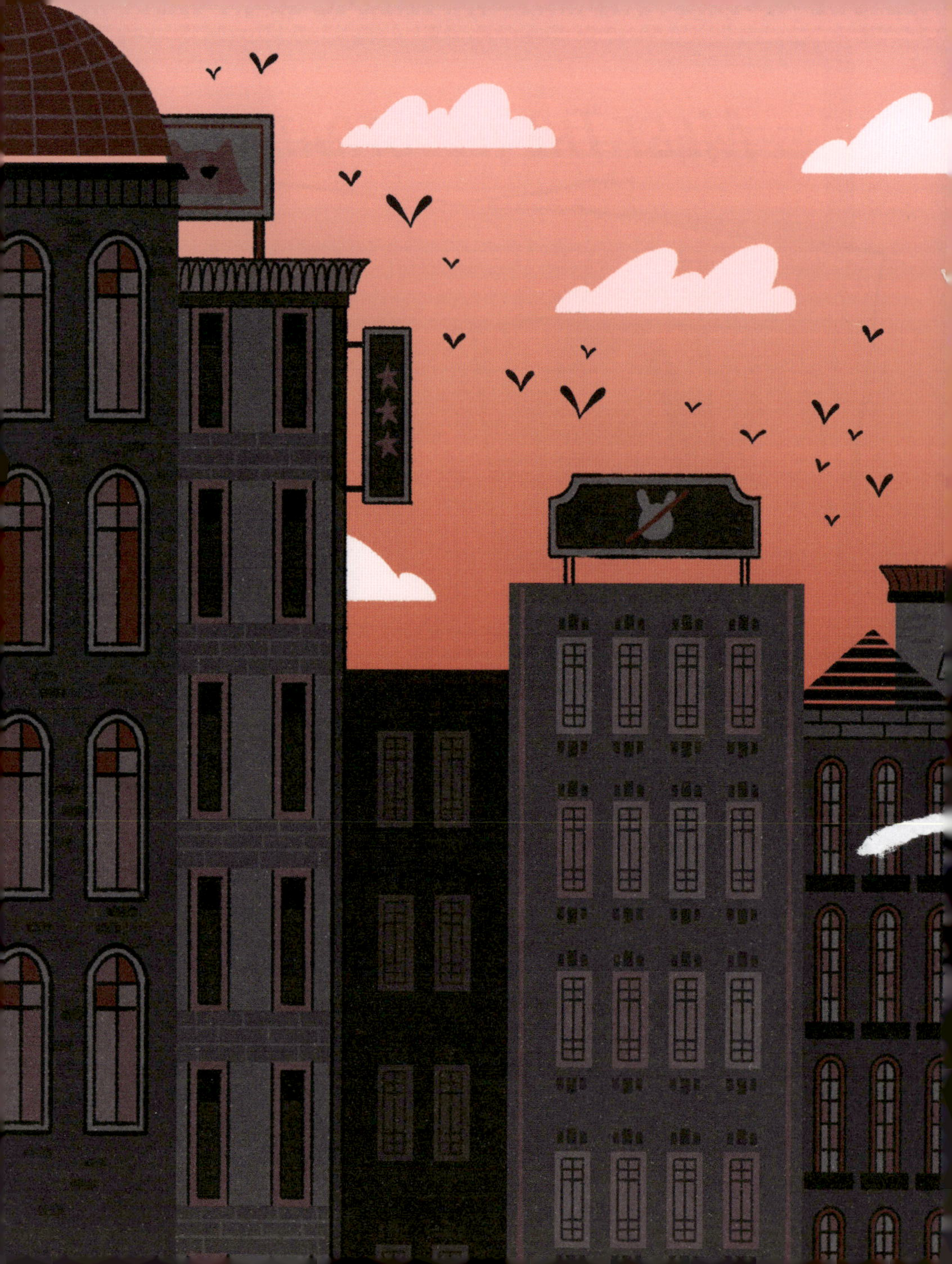